Heavenly
Appointments

A NOVEL ABOUT ABORTION, HEALING & FORGIVENESS

by Karen Leigh

Address all personal correspondence to:

Karen Leigh

P. O. Box 292, Clemmons, NC 27012

Email: KarenLeigh@HeavenlyAppointments.com

Published by:

Pure Heart Publications

Stories that change lives forever

P.O. Box 4260, Cleveland, TN 37320

Phone: 423-478-2843

Website: www.deeperrevelationbooks.org

Email: info@deeperrevelationbooks.org

The fiction division of Deeper Revelation Books

Individuals and church groups may order books from the author directly, or from the publisher. Retailers and wholesalers should order from our distributors. Refer to the Deeper Revelation Books website for distribution information, as well as an online catalog of all our books.

Deeper Revelation Books (and its fiction division, Pure Heart Publications) assists Christian authors in publishing and distributing their books. Final responsibility for design, and doctrinal views, either expressed or implied, belongs to the author.

Dedicated to the

fifty-nine million

and counting ...

Thanks to ...
Janet for pushing me,
Kathy, my sister,
for believing in me,
Diane, Deborah and Colleen
for being so encouraging
and supportive!
A special thanks to ...
Carol

AUTHOR'S NOTE

This book is a work of fiction and is written to highlight the fact that "life begins at conception." Names, characters, incidents and ideas about subjects including dying, the afterlife, Heaven and if the deceased can see or hear the living are products of the author's imagination and are used fictitiously.

However, some references about Heaven are taken from the Bible and are used to help with this narrative and are footnoted where they are found. This book contains a detailed description of an abortion experience and is not intended for younger readers. Any resemblance to actual events or persons, living or dead, is entirely coincidental.

This book is also written to help anyone who has had an abortion, or for anyone who coerced someone to have an abortion, to know that God is a God of forgiveness, grace and love. The author would encourage the reader to keep an open mind about death, dying, angels and Heaven because we won't fully understand them until we experience them for ourselves.

"The boundaries, which divide
Life from Death,
are at best shadowy and vague.
Who shall say where the one ends,
and where the other begins?"

Edgar Allan Poe

TABLE OF CONTENTS

Prologue..13

Chapter 1—Goodbye 15

Chapter 2—Leaving 29

Chapter 3—The Clinic................................... 43

Chapter 4—Arriving....................................... 61

Chapter 5—Loss and Grieving...................... 73

Chapter 6—The Procedure 85

Chapter 7—Starting Over 97

Chapter 8—Mistakes and Sins.................... 111

Chapter 9—Déjà Vu...................................... 123

Chapter 10—Amazing Grace 131

Chapter 11—New Beginnings...................... 143

Chapter 12—Forgiving, Trusting and Healing..... 161

Chapter 13—A Gift From God 167

Chapter 14—The Familiar Girl..................... 173

Chapter 15—A Heavenly Appointment 181

Chapter 16—Reflections 187

Epilogue 189

The Choice.. 201

Endnotes.. 207

PROLOGUE

*"There are far, far better things ahead
than any we leave behind."*

C. S. Lewis

The End

December 31, 2015

The woman's body finally succumbed to the cancer that just two short years ago, invaded and then ravaged her once, very healthy, sixty-four-year-old self. The malignancy arrived as a silent intruder taking up residency in her breast; yet, once detected—just like a squatter—without any right to be there, it refused to leave.

To add insult to injury, the disease was not satisfied to simply exist in a benign state but instead, it maliciously and virulently chose to invade her entire body. A tiny mass was discovered when she'd had a mammogram and after beginning aggressive treatments, which included a double mastectomy, the disease continued to wreak havoc all through her bones, flesh and organs. The cancer stole all semblance of this once physically fit, nutrition conscious and vitamin-dosed woman called Suzanne—taking along with it, her future desires, hopes and dreams.

Three weeks ago, Suzanne was admitted to a local hospice facility to help manage her pain as she approached the end of her illness. Then, just eight days ago, she lapsed into a state of unconsciousness. In the final hours of her life, her breathing became shallow, she inhaled one last time and before she could exhale, she died.

CHAPTER ONE

Goodbye

Jesus told her,
"I am the resurrection and the life.
Anyone who believes in me will live,
even after dying."
John 11:25

Suzanne

December 31, 2015

Suzanne drew her last breath, and instantly she became aware of being pulled out of her lifeless body and lifted up over it. Her senses became sharper as she honed in on her surroundings. Gazing down at her somewhat recognizable self, her body was lying in a bed in a dimly lit room which she characterized as a place for the sick and dying. Her impression was that she had simply shed her skin as she realized that she was still very much alive; it was only her body that was dead.

Curious, she hovered over her motionless body and calmly observed this very familiar shell of herself. She was aware of *someone* or *something* beside her, not human but very real and very present. She experienced the comforting thought that this presence had always been with her, as though assigned to her from her very own conception. The angelic being said nothing, but exuded tranquility, familiarity and safety. What was overwhelming though, was the love acquainted with the being.

As Suzanne silently observed her now dead body, she thought it peculiar to be existing above herself this way and to witness the last moments of her life like a spectator in an arena. From her perspective, she could see herself from every angle. It was as if she were looking at someone else; yet she recognized everything about herself. She was painfully aware of how her once lustrous and salon-styled, auburn-colored hair appeared unkempt as it now revealed secrets of where her once hidden gray remained. She reviewed her body mass taking inventory of how much weight she'd lost. Her almond shaped, dark brown eyes were closed and her rounded face, now pasty and discolored, still bore traces of her once lovely complexion. Despite how thin and sick this identifiable woman appeared to Suzanne—again she reminded herself that it was she, or had been she—there was a satisfaction within her and she was pleased by the thought that she looked as though she were sleeping peacefully. This thought gave her a sense of comfort and even some closure for the body that she once inhabited for more than six decades.

Nevertheless, as she gazed upon herself, for an instant, there was a strong yearning to be back inside herself. Suddenly, a slight panic overcame her, and she lunged toward her body. If she were connected to a heart monitor, a single bleep would have been recorded and the flat line would have jumped. As swiftly as the panic arrived, she remembered the pain and the cancer and how draining these past few months had been. Very quickly, Suzanne was brought back to this new reality she was now experiencing and she was content to merely linger here in this space above herself—looking down upon herself. The angelic being hovered silently beside her, offering reassurance and comfort.

A stark thought flashed through her mind. *Who or what was she now ... without her body?* She felt no different. She likened it to getting older—like when you look in the mirror and see yourself differently than you were ten or twenty years ago, yet, you're still you. Her thoughts were intact, she felt just like herself and she could see and hear. She wondered if she was like the being alongside her? She knew that it reflected a form and a presence, but it was not human. *Then she realized—neither was she—at least not in the way she once knew.*

She remained suspended near the ceiling as she examined her surroundings; it was typical of most hospital rooms with the oversized bed taking up most of the space on the side wall. A nearby over-the-bed table was pushed out of the way and simple belongings rested on it—her reading glasses along with her Bible, some hand lotion and a tube of lipstick. The usual hospital-issued water pitcher sat alongside a half-filled glass of water containing swizzle stick sponges which were used by caregivers to moisten her lips. The curtains that framed the window on the exterior wall were pulled open to display a panoramic night view; the glowing street lamps that lined the sidewalk revealed traces of night mist in their illumination. A countertop filled most of the space on the opposite wall which held a stainless-steel sink with cabinets above and drawers beneath. A small, tired looking Christmas tree fashioned from silver tinsel stood on the countertop; tiny twinkling white lights were strung around it, and a few decorations that she did not recognize dangled from the branches.

As Suzanne scanned the room, she became aware of her daughter, Erin, sitting in a chair, slightly hunched over her dead body, weeping as she held her hand. Suzanne was gripped with a sense of powerlessness as she gazed upon her daughter clinging to an exterior facade, something that merely represented her. The person known to her as *Mom* had left the shell she once occupied. She now existed in a world that was completely invisible and off limits to her daughter.

Suzanne focused on Erin and noted how tired she appeared as she sat, shoulders slumped in the chair beside her mother's bed. Suzanne reflected on memories as thoughts of her daughter flashed through her mind. She admired her daughter like a mother does a child no matter how old they become. At thirty-nine, Erin possessed a quiet strength and an inner beauty earned through a lifetime of hardship.

Her deep-set, bright blue eyes accented with dark eyelashes were filled with tears and her very pale and flawless complexion was now red from crying. Erin normally applied a little make-up to include lipstick, mascara and some light foundation. Tonight, however, she was free of all applications. Erin's dark blonde hair was shoulder-length and almost always worn pulled up in a ponytail, like now. She was dressed in a pair of sweats and a T-shirt complete with moccasin style slippers she always wore in the wintertime. Erin donned a tiny pair of silver hoop earrings and Suzanne was aware that the necklace she wore was the one her father gave her years ago, when she was only fourteen, not long before he died. The serpentine, silver chain held an antique silver heart-shaped locket. Suzanne knew the inscription on the back read, "To My Sweet Girl—Love, Daddy." On the inside of the locket, a picture of Erin and her father had been neatly trimmed to fit in the heart shaped grooves and carefully placed there.

Suzanne glimpsed down and saw Erin's iPhone resting in her lap. She heard it buzz as a text message was recorded in silent mode. She continued surveying the room and detected a styrofoam cup decorated with a holiday motif containing black coffee sitting on the floor near Erin. Based on everything else in the room, she realized it was the holiday season. Suzanne wondered how long it was since she'd been conscious? She thought back, remembering Thanksgiving and how they'd all celebrated over at John and Erin's house along with close friends. It was so good to spend that day with those she loved.

They also celebrated her grandson, Jonathan's, tenth birthday since he was born so close to Thanksgiving. Each one of them made that day so nice for her. The food was delicious—Erin roasted a huge turkey and completed the dinner with corn bread stuffing, fresh green beans, glazed carrots, mashed potatoes and gravy, sweet potato casserole and cranberry sauce, ending with pumpkin pie and whipped cream. Later that afternoon, they presented a two-tiered red velvet layer cake with cream cheese frosting which was decorated with a huge soccer ball and ten candles for Jonathan because he loved both soccer and red velvet cake. Suzanne was only able to eat very small bites of each dish, but she tried not to ruin the gathering for the others with her diminished appetite. So, she made sure she complimented every dish as though she'd eaten heaps.

As she reflected on her Thanksgiving memories with her friends and family, despite all of these details, Suzanne could not remember Christmas. Had Christmas come? She could not remember. She noticed a large wicker basket sitting on the floor; a big red bow was tied to its handle and placed inside was a messy pile of cards and letters.

Suzanne continued surveying the room and saw a beautiful pink and cream poinsettia with tiny yellow centers which filled up the entire corner. Suzanne had always loved plants since she was a young girl and admired how healthy and pretty this one looked. She observed a small candle with a dimly burning flame in a red ceramic votive centered on the window ledge. Suzanne was aware of the scent of evergreen, reminding her of a fresh Christmas tree. The television that was mounted up in the corner of the room was turned on very low to HGTV, one of her favorite channels; yet she could not remember watching anything while she was here.

Suzanne observed Erin's coat and scarf lying in a crumpled heap beside her purse on a chair near the window. She appreciated the beautiful scarf she had painstakingly knit for Erin to wear this winter. At the beginning of her fight with breast cancer, she endured many bouts of chemotherapy and radiation treatments. Suzanne spent many hours going back and forth to the hospital as well as resting at home, so she chose to spend many of those lonely hours knitting to help draw her attention away from the disease as well as the pain and nausea that ensued. Suzanne became so familiar with the yarn she'd selected for this scarf that she paused to admire it once again. She had chosen a chunky, hand-painted wool blend. The colors were beautiful—deep shades of purple and blue along with a hint of scarlet and even some pink. It was so lovely and when Erin wrapped it around her neck for the first time, her face was framed beautifully and it accented her bright blue eyes. Seeing the scarf again made Suzanne grateful to have knit this small token of love for her daughter.

She wondered, *Is today Christmas? Am I dying on Christmas?* And if that were so, she thought, how very sad this would be for her family. The last thing she remembered was being admitted here shortly after Thanksgiving and spending days or weeks as they managed her pain with doses of morphine. Suzanne knew she came here to die. Her life was ending. During the first few days in Hospice Care, she seemed better with the increase in the pain meds. She was coherent and even gained somewhat of an appetite. She conversed with the nurses and was able to give off a pretense of feeling okay when her family or friends came by—if their visits were short enough. But soon, she began to lose her appetite and become lethargic. She slept more. Soon she was sleeping more hours than she was awake. Before long, she became confused upon waking, and somewhere along the way, her caregivers increased the morphine, aware of her obvious need to be out of pain. She slipped away into a state of unconsciousness forgetting about the pain, where she was or why she was there. Suzanne was totally unaware of everything that happened after that.

As she existed in her floating, bodiless state, Suzanne pondered all of this and glanced over at the digital clock on the nightstand. It read 3:33 a.m. She then heard Erin whisper, "Oh Mom, I am going to miss you … " as tears gently fell from her eyes and down her cheeks. Erin's words were expressed to her mother in a heart-wrenching and achingly slow sob. Then she added, "I know you are out of pain now, I know you are okay, Mom." Suzanne curiously watched this drama of her very own life play out in front of her as if she were watching actors on a stage as Erin quietly wept over her. Suzanne heard every word and saw every tear, thinking it so strange to be observing this.

Erin was Suzanne's only child. Overwhelmed with love and reflection, she helplessly watched Erin cry for her while she held her lifeless hand. Suzanne, of course, felt nothing physical. She was out of the shell that once confined and trapped her—she was completely free from the body she was now observing. Yet she still had a soul. She still had emotions, and as a mother, she wanted to go comfort her daughter. She wanted to reach out and tell her that everything would be okay. *But, how could she?*

She continued to linger a while longer, and the thought struck her that life truly wasn't confined to a human body. Life could exist without a body. She was proof of that. She was free of so many things with which a human body entraps you. She felt so liberated. She thought, *This is the afterlife.* And she remained aware of the angelic being that continued to stay close beside her.

As Suzanne continued contemplating all of this, the door swung open and a night nurse quietly entered the room whom she recognized as Cara. She remembered her; she had been so kind. Cara's big golden brown eyes and gentle smile put you at ease right away and her gentle spirit exuded comfort. She was petite with a head full of thick gray hair that she wore in a trendy, short style and, even though she must have been around fifty, her appearance was still youthful. Suzanne was reminded that Cara always treated her with such dignity. Cara walked over to where Erin sat and surveyed Suzanne's rigid body in the bed. She gently touched Erin on the shoulder and whispered, "I'm glad we called, take as long as you need." Then with measured words, she added, "We are filling out the forms and we'll call the coroner when you are ready. Oh, and by the way, your husband phoned the nurse's station. He said you weren't responding to his phone calls or texts—I am pretty sure he will be here in a few minutes." Erin glanced up at Cara momentarily, tears in her eyes, her face red and swollen from crying, then she lowered her gaze back down on her mother and rested it there once again and said wearily, "Thanks Cara, thanks for everything. You've been so great, you have been so kind to all of us, I ... we appreciate all you've done. Mom said nothing but nice things about you." Cara then peered over at Suzanne's corpse lying in the bed and said, "I didn't know her long, but she was one of the good ones. When you've been doing this as long as I have, you get a sense for these things." She then patted Erin's arm and said, "You'll be okay, it will just take some time." Then, just as quietly as she had entered the room, she left, leaving Erin to finish saying goodbye to her mother.

Moments later, the door flung open and John, Erin's husband, came bounding through, hurrying over to Erin's side. He whispered, "Is she ... ?" and his voice trailed off when he saw Erin's tears, his mother-in-law's very still and lifeless body accompanied by the deafening silence in the room. Erin whispered, "Yeah, she's gone." She did not look up to meet John's gaze. She continued answering him, and with a break in her voice, she said, "She's ... gone, John," reaching over to touch a tiny strand of her mother's hair, gently moving it off her face. Tears continued to trickle down Erin's cheeks. Her nose was stopped up, and her hand clutched a wadded-up tissue she was using to dry her dampened face. She continued to answer her husband, "I know she's better off," her voice still wavering, "but I will miss her." Then she smoothed out the blanket spread over her mother's form, took her mother's hand in hers once again, and held it.

John leaned down and put his hand on Erin's shoulder and squeezed it for a second as he gazed down on his mother-in-law. He was at a loss for words and carefully chose how he would answer. He gently and quietly responded to Erin, "Honey," he said, "I'm so sorry, I woke up and realized you were gone. When I couldn't get you to answer, I called the nurses station. I wish you would have woke me up before you left. You knew since Jonathan was staying with Jacob at Catherine's that I could have easily come with you." Erin reached up with her free hand and took hold of John's for a moment and answered him, "I know you would have come if I'd asked you to John, but I wanted to let you sleep; we're all so tired, we've all been through so much these past few weeks." She then turned back toward her mother and touched the ring on her right hand and twisted it around. In a low voice, Erin whispered, "Look how loose her ring is … she lost so much weight; this cancer … it was so awful! Do you think she felt any pain at the end? Do you even think she knew I was here?" She continued gazing on her mother as a single tear fell, dampening the sheet that lay across her mother's lifeless body. Suzanne continued to linger in the space above herself observing her daughter and son-in-law.

This chapter in Erin's life had ended and things would be different now that her mother was gone. Placed nearby was a large, white gift box trimmed with a wide, meshlike gold bow. It contained a beautiful, white linen gown embroidered with lace edging. Erin purchased it at a nearby boutique a few days ago, when she went for a walk. The gown was beautiful and somewhat extravagant for Erin's budget, yet she bought it for her mother to be buried in. She somehow wanted to honor her mom with it … she knew the end was near and wanted her to have something beautiful to wear. Maybe it was foolish, but it was a token of her love. It was tucked away in its tissue lined box. Her mother would never lay her eyes on it.

John drew closer and took Erin's hand once more and squeezed it; he held it tight and then answered her in a meaningful way, "Your mom knew you loved her; you've been here almost every day, especially when she was still conscious. You two had a great relationship these past ten years. It'll be okay Erin, we'll get through this—the three of us together, you still have Jonathan and me. You know your mom is better off, she's out of that awful pain."

John then let go of Erin's hand and walked toward the window feeling powerless and incapable of comforting his wife. He removed his coat, took a deep breath, tossed his coat on the chair along with Erin's things and stared out the window across the street at the Medical Center. He patted his jeans pocket locating his iPhone and removed it; he glanced down to check the time noting that it was a few minutes after 4:00 a.m. He contemplated to himself, *this is going to be a very long day*. It was officially New Year's Eve and this day would be filled with everything but festivities. He certainly wouldn't make it to midnight tonight; 2016 would arrive while he slept unless he could get a nap in. *I'm so glad this is over,* he thought, *it's been so tough on everyone* and he wondered how Erin would handle her grief. He hoped she would be okay. He thought how sad all of this was and strangely, *he still sensed Suzanne's presence in the room like second hand smoke that lingers in the air.*

Leaving

So we fix our eyes not on what is seen,
but on what is unseen,
since what is seen is temporary,
but what is unseen is eternal.

2 Corinthians 4:18, NIV

Suzanne

December 31, 2015

Suzanne invisibly and silently observed her daughter and son-in-law as they each grieved in their own way, but as curious as all of this was for her, she became more aware and more focused on the massive angelic being close beside her. She knew the being was beckoning her to depart from here; it reached out a hand to her and bid her to come, though still silent. She was drawn by the celestial being to leave these troubled, yet somewhat familiar surroundings. Indeed, she felt an overwhelming urgency to go with it. She did not feel afraid even though she sensed she would be going to an unknown place. She agreed with the thought and interpretation and together, they floated up and out of the hospice room.

Upon doing so, Suzanne saw beyond the walls of the room she had been in these past few weeks and observed the ghostly, uninhabited hallways flooded with bright lights. She took inventory of each hospice room with the remaining patients and strangely and interestingly, she saw many more of these massive angelic beings, much like the one with her. They were silently standing by the beds occupied by the sick and dying. She knew they were their guardians and had been with them their entire lives, arriving upon their conception. She, however, continued to float up and out of the hospice care facility.

Once outside, she saw a brightly lit sign that read "Harbour Grace Hospice" and recognized the familiar red brick facade of the building. It was in a busy section of Atlanta surrounded by clusters of medical buildings including the Atlanta Medical Center. The building she was leaving behind was neither inviting nor beckoning. In fact, it gave one the impression of an institution and not a place you would particularly want to visit. She was on Parkway Drive. She recollected that this was where she was brought by the paramedics when she collapsed. She remembered the pain, the fear and a few bits and pieces when she was transported in the ambulance. She painstakingly remembered the chaos and the confusion. Thinking back, it seemed like a long time ago. She recalled what she was doing just before she collapsed—she was on her laptop doing her Christmas shopping—it was early December.

Suzanne was filling out an online order form to purchase gifts for her family, hoping they would arrive in time to wrap up before she became too ill to do so. She knew her time was close and she waited too late to shop. She mistakenly thought she would be able to go to the mall, but her body would not cooperate. She would wake up more and more tired each day. She never felt good enough to leave the house anymore, so she made the decision to do her Christmas shopping online. She was at Nordstrom's website when suddenly she felt an excruciating, sharp pain and grabbed her chest while crying out. Thankfully, her very good friend, Catherine, was visiting and just moments prior, she stepped into the kitchen to make some tea for the two of them. Catherine unmistakably heard Suzanne's cry, came running out of the kitchen and immediately called 911. Suzanne briefly recalled the paramedics arriving, having an oxygen mask placed on her face and being strapped to a gurney as Catherine updated them on her prognosis. She remembered arriving at the Medical Center where she'd been assessed and given a shot of morphine. She was then transferred across the street to Harbour Grace Hospice. One thing she clearly remembered was being out of her body, like now, hovering over the attendants as she watched them care for her. Afterwards, she woke up groggy from a very large dose of pain medication.

Time melted away—the hours blended into days that all seemingly ran together and Suzanne couldn't remember much of the time she'd spent in Hospice Care as the cancer advanced and stole away her last lucid moments. She recollected a few conversations with Erin, discussing things with her that she wanted to say as well as communicating to her the things she *needed* to say. They even discussed her funeral. She was able to convey everything she wanted before she became unconscious. Suzanne remembered rousing and seeing a few close friends and a handful of people from her church, but many of those last days were foggy and unclear. She still did not know what day today was.

Suzanne, now high above the Hospice Care facility was moving quickly through the night air with her angelic escort by her side. She saw places she had visited many times. She was in her city, Atlanta, and saw buildings and streets that brought back memories. She looked down on Centennial Olympic Park, The World of Coca Cola, The Georgia Aquarium and Turner Field, the home of the Atlanta Braves baseball. She reminisced about all the times she'd brought Jonathan and his friend, Jacob, to the aquarium to see the beluga whales, which they called "luga wells" when they were little and learning to talk. The aquarium was completed the month her grandson was born and as soon as he was old enough, she began taking him there. She was just as fascinated as he was by the enormous fish tanks as whales swam over their heads. Later, when they added the dolphin tank, that became Jonathan's favorite exhibit.

As Suzanne lingered here, she noted that it was still dark outside and admired the tiny white lights that graced the trees and buildings as they sparkled prettily in the night mist. It looked cold out judging from the delicate white smoke rising up from the street grates and the lone pedestrian walking down the street all bundled up. Suzanne, however, felt no chill at all and it seemed odd to her that she didn't feel the cold. But, why would she? She had no physical body.

As she moved high above the city, she could see things far off so clearly and soon she was viewing the coastline. She began to recollect beach trips and sunny summer days. She began to reminisce and when she did, she and the angelic being were instantly transported to many familiar places.

First, she found herself at the old beach house on Tybee Island where her grandparents took her when she was a little girl. She loved escaping there in the summers with them. Being with her grandparents was so comforting compared to being at home with her parents. She remembered a feeling of tranquility and safety as she listened to the waves crashing on the shore. She loved walking along this familiar stretch of beach seeing the sudsy water and the shells half-hidden by the sand. She recognized the wrap-around porch with its familiar swing that hung from the wooden ceiling. She visualized herself as a little girl lying across the painted wooden porch playing jacks or working crossword puzzles as her grandmother sat in the nearby swing reading or knitting. She observed the landscape that displayed uneven sand dunes where single plumes of beach grass stood together while leaning in unison; there were big conch shells that lined the sandy path and stepping stones placed strategically on the path leading up to the old house. She remembered everything about this old familiar house and it was just like she was coming for a visit.

The large braided rugs in every room warmed up the old oak wood floors. She recalled the cozy, inviting kitchen that she and her grandmother baked in. She remembered how she used to love cooling herself beneath the large ceiling fan after sweating in the scorching summer heat, which made the screened-in back porch one of her favorite places.

Glancing toward the guest room, she thought about the many hours she'd spent in this room she'd always claimed as her own with the pale-yellow walls. Twin white wrought-iron headboards leaned flimsily against the wall; blue and white quilts were neatly folded across the bottom half of each bed with fluffy white pillow shams and tossed in front were tiny red pillows embroidered with white sailboats. She eyeballed the tall blue and white striped floor lamp that reminded her of a lighthouse. Over in the corner of the room was a small white wicker rocking chair with an oversized red and white checkered cushion seat that she always thought looked like a tablecloth one would use for a picnic. The chair was so comfy; she would sit and read her mysteries in it for hours. She loved visiting her grandparents here at the beach house and had so many fond memories of making peach cobbler with her grandmother after stopping at the produce stands along the way where they would purchase Georgia peaches, green beans, tomatoes, okra and Vidalia onions. Each time she went, it always felt like home. Suzanne didn't know how long she stayed there reminiscing but she sensed that time was not something she needed to concern herself with anymore. She was continuously aware of the massive angelic being by her side.

She paused and began to think about the present and instantly, she was again floating in the sky and before she knew it, she was transported to her own home with all its familiar surroundings. It was uninhabited. She never remarried after losing Paul. This was the house she'd purchased after Erin left home—it was practical, small and cozy. Previously, she, Paul and Erin lived in a larger home in the suburbs but this little cottage was even further out from the congested city of Atlanta, and she loved the quiet neighborhood.

Suzanne's thoughts raced back to the struggles she faced so many years ago, after Paul was killed that fateful night in June and how hard it was the first year when Erin was so young—only fourteen. She remembered how in her stages of grieving, she'd given up on taking care of Erin those first few months. She relived and reviewed all the memories as they quickly rushed in on her ... getting through the grief, blaming God, the struggles and the guilt ... she remembered everything. She thought about how she used the insurance money to make the mortgage payments as an attempt to remain in their family home. For some reason, it was important to her to remain in the home they were last complete as a family and which held some of their happiest moments together. She wanted Erin to have stability, even if it was all a facade. She did not want to relocate so quickly after Paul's death, plus it was a terrible economy. Thinking back, she contemplated that maybe her decision to stay in that house was part of the reason Erin experienced so many problems after Paul's death.

She had undeniably been able to hold things together financially for a while with the insurance proceeds and then later with the steady employment she'd found. She continued teaching after the cancer diagnosis until she was forced into early retirement at sixty-three when she and her doctor came to the realization that it was not going into remission.

Reflecting back on it all, Suzanne remembered when she had *not* held it together emotionally for so many months after Paul died. She had lost at least six months of her life as well as Erin's. It took her such a long time to finally heal from her pain and it affected Erin in the most tragic way.

A few years later, when Erin left for college and began her career, Suzanne relocated here. As she drank in the memories of this home she'd resided in for over twenty years now, she was still thankful for it and comforted that she decided on this particular house in this particular neighborhood.

She inspected her private garden out back where she'd spent so many hours planting annuals and perennials, and every summer, she would grow as many tomatoes as her tiny space would allow. Suzanne had a favorite spot on the porch where many mornings she would sit in a comfy chair drinking coffee and spending time praying. This home was perfect for a single woman such as herself especially since it was all one level, brick and very low maintenance. She admired it once again remembering just how much she loved the colors she chose the last time she'd redecorated the inside. Suzanne loved indoor plants and when she surveyed the indoors, she was painfully aware that they were looking dry and in need of watering.

She continued examining the surroundings and spotted her favorite brown leather chair and draped across its back was her favorite afghan; she spent so many hours in this comfortable spot reading, knitting and watching TV—especially the last year. It seemed odd to be here like this. But as much as she reminisced and took it all in, she did not feel drawn to stay. It was simply closure for her. As she continued observing this space, Suzanne had the sobering thought that the owner was now deceased. She continued to be mindful of the angelic being that lingered nearby.

Suzanne's thoughts then turned to Catherine and instantly she was in her home. She found herself gazing down on her friend of twenty plus years as she slept peacefully beside her husband, Bill. Catherine had been the best friend anyone could have. She showed up at just the right time in her life. Suzanne always felt that Catherine was an angel sent by God to help her through some of the worst times in her life. She was so grateful for her.

Catherine's cell phone rested on the bedside table. She knew Catherine typically did not take her phone to bed and Suzanne figured it was only there because she was waiting for Erin to call her to share her mother's demise. Their little dog, a beagle named Queenie, roused and gazed up at her in the darkened room, then whined a little as she sensed Suzanne's presence.

Suzanne moved past the master bedroom to the extra bedroom and observed the two little boys sleeping soundly; her grandson, Jonathan, along with Catherine's grandson, Jacob, lay snoozing on bunk beds. Jacob, nine, was splayed out on the top bunk and Jonathan, ten, was curled up on the bottom. They were the best of friends. She and Catherine were blessed to have daughters who had been close and then grandsons born within a few months apart and luckily for all of them, they'd all become good buddies.

It was a lot of fun for them to hang out together on special occasions and celebrate the boy's birthdays with each other. Suzanne wondered when Jonathan last visited her. Did he come to see her in Hospice Care? She did not remember.

She thought back and remembered when Catherine decorated this special room for her little grandson, Jacob, when he was just a toddler. Catherine certainly had a knack for decorating. She selected a border consisting of basketballs, footballs and soccer balls and installed it above the white chair rail that rested on a pewter colored wall. The comforters that now warmed the two little boys were navy blue, and tossed aside in the corner of the room were decorative pillow shams in a geometric pattern of navy blue, white and yellow. There was a little distressed wooden desk painted gray with a matching wooden chair complete with a coordinating soft cushion. Nearby were three rows of plastic crates stacked on top of each other in white, blue and yellow that created six cubbies overflowing with toys and games these two little boys shared and played with over the years. Their iPad minis were lying on the floor beside the bed, and nearby was a TV on a stand connected to a PlayStation. Over in the corner of the room stood a floor lamp and beside it were two large denim bean bag chairs with kid-sized indentations complete with game controllers resting on them. It was a fun room for these two little friends and they had enjoyed romping and playing in it for years. It seemed Jonathan and Jacob fell asleep and left all their clothes and toys scattered across the room. She paused, looked at the boys sleeping and then her gaze rested on Jonathan, whom she thought looked so much like her husband, Paul—his grandfather, whom he had never met. She thought about all the emotional ups and downs Erin had been through and how thankful Erin and John were when they finally conceived a child, this precious little boy, Jonathan. She and Erin previously wondered if she would ever have a successful pregnancy after what transpired in her youth.

After all her reminiscing, the angelic being beckoned her once more to come farther to an even higher space that was vast and boundless. With no reservation or apprehension, Suzanne followed; yet once she crossed over into this new space, she realized without a doubt she could not go back. She could no longer return to any of the recognizable or familiar places she just visited and left behind.

She could not go back to the beach house, her

home or her friend's home. Would she ever see her friend again? Or her grandson? She couldn't go back and see her daughter, Erin holding her hand and crying. She could not *will* herself back to her very own body. Everything earthly was now out of her reach—*even her body*.

Suzanne apprehensively concluded that she must accept this realization and upon doing so, the angelic being brought her comfort and reassurance. The communication between them was intimate and had seemingly lasted a lifetime—*her lifetime*. It did not seem odd to her that this angelic being was beside her guiding her along; it felt so natural to her. And the angelic being was familiar with her. The Being did not just arrive upon the death of her body, but had been with her since the moment she was conceived. She was mindful and aware of that truth.

Suzanne began traveling with her companion through the atmosphere where thousands upon thousands of stars shone, lighting up the vast darkness. She perceived that she was in the Milky Way galaxy, a tiny corner of the massive universe. She could see planet earth and the remaining planets in this solar system.

Instantly, she was traveling farther away from the Milky Way galaxy. She discerned that she just traveled light years away from her former earthly home. She passed through galaxy upon galaxy and when she did, she saw that each of them contained thousands upon thousands of stars and planets that were never detected or discovered by any telescope or intelligence from planet earth. She was in awe of the most astounding light show that no planetarium production could ever duplicate; she was amazed by shooting stars that danced in the night sky and comets as they streaked by while each one performed on this universal landscape. She was exploring a cosmos yet to be discovered—exploding stars, black holes and dark energy. She viewed God's creation on a whole different level while comprehending that this was only the first layer. *There would be so much more to come.*

Suzanne understood that she was just a tiny speck in a massive, God-created universe. She became astutely aware of how minuscule she was. Yet as enormous and massive as all this infinite expansiveness was that now enveloped her, *she still knew she was somebody. She was a somebody without a body.*

The angelic being bid her once more to come and follow. She continued moving through the boundless and limitless space. Then suddenly, she was overtaken by what was in an indescribable darkness. There was no light source from anywhere. She had just travelled through the night sky with the moon, the stars and even the planets lighting up the darkness; but now she was in a darkness that was totally black with no hope of any light: *utter, outer darkness.* There was nothing to compare it to. It was as if a curtain just closed on the entire universe to block everything out. Yet, before she could even think to be afraid, she sensed she was moving through what she believed was a tunnel. She felt herself—whatever there was of herself—being propelled faster and faster to a speed she knew she'd never experienced. She briefly thought of the sensation of flying in an airplane and how it feels when you take off and experience the power of becoming airborne. That was only for an instant. This speed went far beyond that. It was indescribable. The tunnel was a passageway leading to where she was going, or so it seemed. She became aware that she was entering a corridor of some sort.

Momentarily, she began to hear music resonating in the distance. It was the most comforting and beautiful sound she had ever heard … millions of voices accompanied by musical instruments, some recognizable and some were not. As she continued moving rapidly through the darkness, she saw a very faint light. There was a glow around it and it flickered like a candle. As she drew closer to it, the glimmering light became brighter and brighter. This radiant light possessed a warmth and a love that totally overpowered her. She felt as drawn to this light as the proverbial moth to a flame. Then suddenly, the brightness and the illumination of the light became blinding. She felt herself being sucked "through" something such as a vacuum. It was a barrier of some sort and instantaneously she broke through to another side. Where? She did not know.

And just as quickly as this journey began, it was over, and there was a sense of calm—like the tranquil feeling of holding your newborn baby after hours of labor while at the same time perceiving that a whole new reality waits on the horizon.

CHAPTER 3

The Clinic

God made me in my mother's womb,
and he also made them;
the same God formed both of us
in our mothers' wombs.
Job 31:15, NCV

Before I formed you in the womb I knew you,
before you were born I set you apart.
Jeremiah 1:5, NIV

Erin
Wednesday, January 15, 1992

Fifteen-year-old Erin reluctantly sat in the waiting room alone. Her appointment was for one o'clock. She left her school in the suburbs where she lived and took the bus all the way into Atlanta. She exited the bus, book bag in tow, at the Chamblee-Dunwoody Road bus stop and hesitantly ventured down the street to where the clinic that she so desperately sought after was located. It was a poor and neglected neighborhood, and Erin was uneasy when she stepped down from the safety of the bus into this unchartered and unfamiliar territory. She continued moving closer to the address she had jotted down on a single slip of paper from her 10th grade, college-ruled notebook.

When Erin finally phoned the clinic seeking information about a free pregnancy test, she still hoped that the previous one she took in the stall of the girl's bathroom would turn out to be a false reading. The lady who'd answered the phone was informative and naturally put Erin at ease saying, "Yes, honey, we can help you." She then proceeded to ask Erin whether she had taken a pregnancy test? When Erin answered, "yes" and then another "yes" to confirm that it was positive, the woman persuaded Erin to come to the clinic as easily as giving candy to a baby. "Why don't I just go ahead and make you an appointment, sweetheart; we'll give you another pregnancy test and if that one is positive, the doctor can see you right then." Speaking in her accented southern drawl she added, "It's a very simple procedure, and it will only take a few minutes." She then enthusiastically continued informing Erin, "You will feel fine by the next day. Don't you worry about a thing except getting here. What day is good for you?"

And so, she found the clinic, entered, checked in with the receptionist and located a seat to wait. Erin sat alone and thought back, as soon as she had seen the plus sign on the pregnancy test, she began to fantasize about marrying Michael and having his baby. But now she realized she was just a stupid, silly girl who knew nothing about boys. Instead of realizing her hopes and dreams, she now sat nervous in an uncomfortable plastic chair positioned along the wall in the waiting room of a place called "The Women's Clinic." This is where Michael suggested she go, and he provided her with the phone number.

Erin sat, hands folded in her lap anxiously waiting in an accurately described room of an inaccurately described building realizing just how scared and truly alone she was. She certainly didn't feel like a woman; she felt like a little girl, and she was—just fifteen this past September. She didn't want to be here anymore than she wanted to leave; because if she left, she would have an even bigger problem—a baby to take care of. Erin was alone and afraid. Michael reluctantly offered to drive her to the clinic but she knew he wasn't sincere; he didn't care about her anymore, maybe he never did. He got what he wanted. The only thing Michael cared about now was making sure she got rid of *her problem*, not his problem, but *hers*— that's what he said. She did not think he would be like that, especially not in the beginning when they first began dating.

He obviously was not concerned for her at all. It was so clear to her now, so she refused his offer to drive her to this place. She instead opted to deal with this nightmare that began several months ago independent of him and on her own. She left her house that morning with confidence figuring she could do this alone but now, she wasn't so sure. She went to school and soon faked an illness. She then left the campus making her way to the bus stop; but with each unfamiliar step she took, she begun to lose the feeling that she could do this all by herself.

Erin needed a way to pay for it though, so she certainly did not turn down the money Michael provided. By now, she was upset and annoyed with him, so she figured he could at least pay for it … *pay to get rid of it. Where else would she get that kind of money?* She certainly would not get it from her mother. They both knew that. Michael gave her $400 in cash and told her he was really sorry. He said this was the best thing for the both of them and to call him *after*.

But Erin knew he wasn't sincere about hearing from her again. Michael's only concern was heading off to college next fall. Erin thought how extremely lucky he was to be leaving. It would be a whole new beginning for him; she still had two more years of high school. From the moment she'd first told him, he stopped taking her out as before. The only time he called since was to tell her about this stupid place, ask her a bunch of questions, and then he called her back once more to find out what day she was going to the clinic. She could tell how relieved he was when she told him she made the appointment. Then, they met once more so he could give her the fake ID card and the money. He didn't kiss her or hug her like he always did before. He was cold and uncaring, and she couldn't understand why. She called him a few more times prior to today hoping that he would want to hear from her, but lately he was always busy with his friends. She finally realized he wanted nothing more to do with her. She could not believe how stupid she was. Yep, she was a stupid, silly girl.

Erin was lost in her thoughts as she sat in these

troublesome surroundings waiting with all the other women, or girls really, who looked just like she did— scared, nervous? Most of the girls seemed to be around her age, but none of them were talking to one another. A couple of girls sat with their boyfriends. Erin assumed they were boyfriends as they were holding hands. One girl sat beside a girlfriend or maybe a sister, but most of the girls sat alone with their heads down, hunched over looking at magazines, looking off into space or staring at the TV that was mounted in the corner of the room. The channel was turned to the popular soap opera, *All My Children*, which to even fifteen-year-old Erin, seemed ironic. She noticed one girl undoubtedly had her mother sitting next to her, at least Erin guessed it was her mother based on the way they were at ease with one another. Erin wondered how did she persuade her mom to agree to this? What mother would want this for a daughter? Erin knew that if her mom knew, she would not let her do this. Her mom was such a mess right now though. She'd been totally out of it since her dad died. Yet, she didn't want to think about that right now; it was too painful.

Erin was so relieved when the receptionist did not look too closely at the picture on the driver's license Michael borrowed, or truth be told, *stolen* from his older brother's girlfriend's wallet. How could the receptionist not have known that the picture wasn't her? How could she not have known that Erin was really only fifteen? How could any of these girls be old enough? Very few of them looked eighteen to her—Erin was tall for her age but still, she didn't look eighteen. It was so obvious. But thank God nobody said anything. All she wanted to do was get this over with and go home. "Ashley," a voice announced.

Erin had thought through this a thousand times. She was confident she could go through with it. She knew it would be over soon, and she would return home; she'd be back home in the safety of her bedroom that she and her mom decorated together just last summer. Erin couldn't believe how many things had changed in just a few short months. How did she get here? How did it all end up like this? Just last year she and her daddy were shopping together at the mall and going to movies. She and her mom were picking out paint colors for her new bedroom. They even bought a stuffed animal for her bed. It was a big white bear, and she still hugged it every night. She felt like she was living a whole different life now.

Erin continued to reminisce about her mom and her dad and their old life. But soon, she forced herself to snap out of it before she could fantasize too much about how things could have been. She was brought back to her present reality as her thoughts trailed off. Erin was convinced if she could just go through with the motions of this afternoon, she would soon be home lying on her bed doing her homework and listening to music. Her favorite song right now was Amy Grant's hit, "Baby, Baby" but it kept reminding her of *her baby*. Would she ever be able to listen to that song again without remembering today?

She supposed her mom would never find out. In fact, Erin did not think her mother cared a thing about her anymore. Her mother knew nothing about her life these days; she never asked. Her mom didn't seem to care about anything at all anymore, including herself. Erin came to the realization as she sat there that she hadn't just lost her dad; she had lost her mom too.

Her mom was such a loser now. She wouldn't get up off the couch. She sat on the sofa all day with the TV on. She wouldn't even cook dinner. She used to love coming home from school finding her mom in the kitchen conjuring up a new recipe. She and her dad would make fun of her mom's organic, healthy recipes, but most of the time, they were actually pretty good. She wished she would cook now. Instead, she would order a pizza or go to drive through restaurants like McDonald's or Taco Bell, which in the past Erin would have loved but now a drive through or fast food restaurant simply represented her mother's inability to function. She bought TV dinners and frozen foods, she didn't even shop at the grocery store during the day like normal mothers. Instead, she would go out to the stores that were open at night and bring the bags in like she was a drug dealer or something. The food she bought was mostly processed and already prepared.

Erin was always looking for something decent to eat, especially lately; she was always hungry and never seemed to be able to find what she craved. Sometimes, Erin would make something for the both of them and take it to her mom as she sat merely existing on the sofa. She quietly hoped her mom would ask her a question or start up a conversation about school or anything for that matter. She wished she would ask her to sit down and eat with her, but she never did. Her mom just acted like a zombie and there was a hollow look about her.

Erin didn't feel like her mother was trying hard enough, and she looked like crap. She used to be so pretty and liked to shop, have her hair done and wear makeup. Lately she looked and acted like a mental patient. Erin guessed her mom had truly lost it, and she was beginning to feel like she had too.

She knew her Dad was never coming back and her mom had completely checked out. She knew her mom was sad. Her weight loss made her look even more so. Erin felt really bad for her—but her mother wasn't the only one in pain. Erin missed her dad so much. She missed him so much it hurt. Erin *needed* someone. Michael filled that void for her—up until now. And now, sadly, Erin had no one—again. *Nothing was the same anymore.*

Erin thoughts flashed to last summer, she and her mom were waiting for her dad to come home so the three of them could go out to dinner. It was the beginning of the weekend, and they all loved eating out together on Friday nights. She reminisced back to that night. There were so many things she wanted to talk to her dad about, but she was saving it up for Sunday. Sunday afternoons were always their special time together. She loved those couple of hours they would spend with one another. They called it their father/daughter date. On one of those outings, they picked out a silver locket. Later, her dad purchased it, had it engraved and then gave it to her for her fourteenth birthday. Since then, Erin always wore it. She never removed it, not even to bathe. That was not that long ago ... she missed her dad so much. Erin reached up and fingered the locket and moved it back and forth on its chain, as she continued to reminisce about her dad. One of the last movies Erin remembered watching with him was, "Back to the Future." They both loved it. She now sat in this unfamiliar place thinking how she wished she could go backward or forward in time and find her dad. *Where was he?*

As her mother and she waited for her dad to arrive home, their stomachs growled as they complained about him always being late. Then everything changed for them that Friday evening in June. They'd moved to a new home a few months prior and both mother and daughter were eager to check out the neighborhood pool together that day and hopefully make some new friends. So far, they met one family who had a daughter Erin's age, Christy, and her mother Catherine. They seemed to hit it off great as they talked a little and soon realized they attended the same church. Of course, ever since Erin's father died, they had not set foot in a church, and Erin missed it. What on earth was going on she wondered? *Why,* she thought, *did her mother and father take her to church every single Sunday before he died and now she and her mother never went?* She remembered the pastor talking about God helping you through hard times and things like that. So why didn't they go anymore? She did not understand.

Erin and her mom spent a couple of hours together

at the pool that day and when they came home, they showered and changed into pretty sun-dresses her mom purchased at the mall earlier that summer—perfect for a night out and showing off their suntans. Despite the sunscreen that her mother always made her apply, and keep applying, Erin's nose was a little red as were her shoulders and her mother fussed at her for not using enough. Erin was starving, she had recently gone through a growth spurt and was now an inch or two taller than her mother. Although she still wore a couple of sizes smaller than her mother, boys began to notice her, and she liked that. That was the main topic of some of the questions she wanted to talk to her dad about when they would get together on Sunday.

Erin wanted to ask him how to choose a boy who would treat her good, like he treated her mom. She thought her father could help her with this advice. She knew he would tell her she was too young, but she hoped he would be willing to give her a little bit of wisdom concerning this. He was good like that. Erin spent a lot of time getting ready for that night working extra hard blow drying her hair and adding lip gloss and mascara to her sun-kissed face. She couldn't wait to go eat; it was one of her favorite things to do with her mom and dad and they all agreed on their favorite Mexican restaurant. Erin was thinking about those chips and the chunky red salsa.

That night, she and her mother naturally both assumed that her dad was running a little late which wasn't unusual for him. But six o'clock turned into 6:30, and then close to 6:45, her mom received a phone call, *that miserable phone call*. Erin and her mother rushed off together to the hospital and that was it. Nothing was ever the same again. Nothing would ever be the same. She was only fourteen when she lost her daddy and today, she needed him more than ever—but he was gone. She missed him so much. She wouldn't even be in this miserable place if it weren't for these past few months.

When Erin met Michael, only a few months had passed since her dad's death. She met him in the fall of her sophomore year after a football game on a Friday night. She had just turned fifteen in September and her daddy died the previous summer; her heart was numb, and she was feeling lost. She and two girlfriends were at an after-game party somewhere on a dirt road. There was a bonfire and a keg of beer. Tons of kids were running around in the dark laughing and joking and seemingly having a good time; but Erin was feeling nothing but out of place and uncomfortable. Her girlfriends, Christy and Heather, basically dragged her here and then disappeared.

Erin stood alone leaning against somebody's car whom she did not know and a guy named Michael simply walked up and began a conversation with her. It turned out to be his car she was leaning on. He was older, a senior and really nice and really cute. He spent the entire evening talking to her. He was drinking a beer from the keg and Erin was uncomfortable with that, but he did not seem drunk to her. A drunk driver killed her dad, so Erin had a huge problem with any kind of alcohol ever since that night. She had never tasted alcohol. After talking a little while, Michael began to ask her a few questions. She reluctantly told him about losing her dad and what happened that past summer and he seemed genuinely sorry and acted like he really cared. He said, "I don't know what I would do if I lost my dad like that" and "this must be so hard for you." For the first time since her dad died, Erin finally felt that someone empathized with her. She felt that someone finally acknowledged even just a little bit of her pain. Christy's mom was nice to her and seemed concerned but she didn't know her very well and Christy was nice too when they talked about it, but she couldn't sincerely understand what Erin was feeling. Yet, there was something about this guy, Michael, which caused her to feel like he understood her pain.

Michael soon excused himself informing her he'd be back in a few minutes. He walked away, and she wondered if he had disappeared forever just like her dad. However, he soon returned holding two cans of coke dripping with freezing cold water. He offered her one and Erin thought, because of that, he respected her feelings about the beer he was previously drinking, and she thought, *Maybe he likes me?* He complimented her that night on her outfit and her hair. He even asked her about the locket she wore. They seemed to click and before she left the party, he asked her for her phone number and he called her the very the next day. There was a second line in her bedroom, a teenager's telephone, and soon she was talking to him late into the night, several nights a week.

Very soon, they began going out after school and when she was with him, she finally felt like she mattered to someone again; he listened to what she said—*and, he owned a car.* Her mom never cared where she was anymore. Erin was surprised at all the freedom she now had. She loved it. All she did was write a note letting her mom know she would be late because she was "studying with a friend," "going to the library," "taking a test" or something lame like that. Her mother didn't keep up with anything anymore; she never knew when there were football games or any kind of school events. Before her dad died, her mother kept up with everything; she'd even volunteered at her old school and before, she would ask Erin tons of questions about school, the teachers and the kids. But not anymore, and truth be told, Erin missed all of that. She wished for someone to care about her and now, someone did. *Michael did.* At first, they spent a lot of time together with Michael's friends and out at public places, they would go to McDonald's after school and order fries and share them along with a coke or they would get a milkshake—chocolate for her, vanilla for him. Soon though, they were spending time alone— lots of time alone.

Then that afternoon when Erin told Michael she was pregnant, he turned as white as a sheet and instantly became so upset with her. She couldn't understand—*Why was he mad at her?* He was the one who talked her into it and kept taking her to the places they could be alone. And now he was blaming her? After days of talking, him asking her questions and her answering them, including all his accusations such as her not being on the pill and making her to feel like it was *all her fault*, he told her very matter-of-factly that she needed to have an abortion. He would be gone before this baby would ever be born. "When is 'it' due?" he asked her over and over, making her feel like he hadn't been involved in any of it. Erin knew that college would begin in August for Michael, and she tried to calculate when she'd stopped having her period and figure it up. She didn't know how to figure it up except to count nine months. But based upon all of the alone time they'd had these last few weeks—coupled with the fact that her last period was some time in November—she thought their baby would come in September, her own birth month. *And Michael was right—he would be gone.* But there would be no baby because she was sitting here in this clinic waiting for some unknown doctor to sweep it away … *What do they do with it?* she wondered.

The clinic's pregnancy test was positive also. After she received those results, she was instructed to "Wait for the doctor."

Besides Michael, Erin felt close to one other person, Christy, who she spent several hours a week with. Christy's mom, Catherine, would pick her up from school each morning. She thought Christy's mom was an okay lady. When Erin's dad died, Christy's mom began offering her rides to school and inviting her to church. They took her to the beach in July for a week. Christy's mom had begun asking Erin lots of questions lately though, and Erin hated that. She would ask her over and over how her mom was doing. She would ask Erin why she didn't need a ride home every day. The woman was a little too nosy for her.

But Christy was a nice girl and Erin liked her. Erin told Christy about Michael and how crazy she was about him after that night they went to the party together. She told her about dating him. But telling Christy about this, a baby? No way, that would be much too hard. Everything in her whole life was just too difficult. Erin tried to talk to Christy about her dad a few times after he died and tell her how much she missed him but she found she just couldn't do it. Christy could not understand; *she still had her dad.*

She and Christy watched the movie "Father of the Bride" over the Christmas holidays and Erin cried and cried when she returned home to the safety and comfort of her bedroom. She wanted her daddy back so bad. Christy couldn't understand her pain. No one did. At first, Michael let her talk a little bit about how much she missed her dad. But when she'd cried, that was when he'd begun to comfort her and things went too far.

On the other hand, Erin complained a lot to Christy about her mom and how she never did anything. She could confide to Christy how she hated the way her mother was acting now. When Christmas came, her mother did nothing like she had done in previous years and Erin was heartbroken that all their traditions were left behind like something precious that was totally forgotten. Talking bad to Christy about her mom was pretty safe territory because Christy complained about her mom too. But now, Erin was pregnant, and she didn't have anyone she could talk to about it. She knew there was no one who would understand this.

Secretly, she hoped Michael would say, "Let's get married." She could leave her mom, leave school and leave the past behind. She could start a new life with Michael and their baby. She could name it "Paul" after her dad if it was a boy and "Paula" or "Polly" if it was a girl. But who was she kidding? Michael had been accepted to a state school and would begin college next fall. He was so lucky. Michael's whole life was ahead of him. He would not let her ruin it for him. He told her that a baby would ruin his life and hers too. He stated to her very cooly that this was the best way. He even challenged her with the idea that they made abortion legal just so people's lives wouldn't be ruined by having babies too young. He said they passed a law called *Roe v. Wade* in 1973 and it was supposed to help women who did not want to have a baby. She supposed it was true. He seemed to know what he was talking about. But still, Erin wished … she hated that this was the only way and, *If it was legal, she wondered, why did she need the fake ID?*

Michael
January, 1991

Michael kept thinking about how bad he screwed up after Erin told him her horrible news. When he first met her, he thought she was the sweetest, prettiest girl. He really liked being with her and he loved how it felt to be seen with such a beautiful girl. The night he saw Erin leaning on his car, she just seemed so sad and he was momentarily taken off guard by her eyes that seemed too innocent; instantly, he wanted to be her friend and get to know her better. He couldn't believe she was only a sophomore. She was gorgeous with her long blonde hair, blue eyes and long tanned legs. He thought she looked like a model, and she was just so innocent. He knew *he* was not innocent or a virgin anymore, he'd had his moments with girls, and he regretted a lot of things.

Yet despite all the girls he'd dated and slept with, he had never really experienced an honest relationship with anyone, at least not anyone that he thought would last, and that is something he was looking for, a relationship that would last. He thought to himself, *If only he hadn't pushed Erin into sleeping with him, maybe they could have experienced a real love relationship that would have gone somewhere. Maybe she would have been someone he could have built a future with. Instead, she had to go and get herself pregnant, and what in the world was he supposed to do about that? He was still just a kid himself, only eighteen, and he was leaving for college in a few months. If his parents found out, they would freak out.*

At first, when he and Erin began spending time together and getting closer to each other, he thought she needed him. He liked her a lot; they hung out together and did a lot of talking and getting to know each other. Once he realized he was her first boyfriend and obviously, a virgin, he wanted to sleep with her, but he didn't think she was stupid enough to go and get herself pregnant. After they slept together, there was an emotional bond between them and he really did feel something special for Erin, not like the other girls that he used for casual sex. Forget about that now, *she was not going to ruin his life.*

When Erin told him she was pregnant, she looked at him with her bright blue eyes and seemed so hopeful. *But for what he wondered?* He felt awful about it. *But seriously?* She was so heartbroken when he told her there was no way he wanted a baby. He always wondered about her mom, he couldn't figure that one out. *Where was she all these months they dated?* Erin never talked about her and if anything did come up, Erin would just say, "She's out of it." And what did that even mean? The most important thing for him to do now was to make sure she gets rid of it. He stole his older brother's girlfriend's ID right out of her purse when she left it in the living room. That was easy. He withdrew the money he needed from his savings account hoping his mom wouldn't see his statement the next time it came and ask questions. If she did, he would figure out something to tell her. The hard part now would be making sure Erin went through with it. God, he hoped she would get rid of it. *What choice did he really have?*

Arriving

> *We know that God,*
> *who raised the Lord Jesus,*
> *will also raise us with Jesus*
> *and present us to himself*
> *together with you.*
>
> 2 Corinthians 4:14

Suzanne

Eternity A.D.

Suzanne was outside of time between the passageway that separated earth from Heaven.

She died at 3:33 on December 31st, 2015, in a Hospice Care facility while her daughter, Erin, sat by her bedside holding her hand. She witnessed all of this when her spirit left her body. She was now somewhere that was not like anything she had ever known or experienced.

She saw a path and as she began to venture along this path, it became more and more narrow.[1] She continued moving on the path, still aware of the massive angelic being that remained close by her side. At the end of this narrow path, she saw a small passageway; it was a gate. It was not open, and she wondered how she would enter. As Suzanne approached the gate, she was conscious of a covering over her like a cloud that moved when she moved. It was a covering of blood, not hers. Suzanne understood that it was the blood of Jesus and upon that knowledge, the small gate opened right up, and she proceeded right through. The gate closed instantly behind her.

Suzanne was not afraid. An indescribable peace enveloped her. She knew she was welcome. In fact, she now possessed knowledge she previously did not have and knew she was expected. She sensed abundant love, peace and acceptance and her entire being breathed in this knowledge. She possessed a feeling of belonging and of coming home. She also experienced the excitement one feels upon arriving somewhere they'd never been but always wanted to go. Mostly, she sensed she was finally home after a long and wearisome journey and everything hard was now behind her.

Suzanne was in Heaven—in the very presence of God, the Father—*her Father* was the light here. There would be no more night, the light came from God and there was no more need for the sun or the moon or the stars.[2]

> *There shall be no more night, and they will not need lamps or sunlight, because the Lord God will be their light.* Revelation 22:5

She could hear singing and it sounded like a billion voices proclaiming the Holiness of God all in unison.

The voices singing were angels and they continued to bless God and His Son, Jesus. The singing was the entire backdrop of this unfamiliar, yet exciting landscape.

The sounds Suzanne heard were like oceans crashing on the shore or distant thunder in the sky and she could hear voices singing, "Holy, Holy, Holy, to the Lord God Almighty." They never stopped singing or praising God. She somehow knew that this had been going on since the beginning of time without ceasing.

There was a glorious throne and Someone was sitting on it and He gleamed like precious stones and around the throne there was a radiant rainbow.[3] From the throne came flashes of lightning, rumblings and peals of thunder.[4] There was also a fragrance that surrounded her; it was a beautiful aroma that went right up to the throne of God. She knew this essence was the prayers of God's people and it lingered here before Him night and day.[5]

The angelic being who escorted her from her deathbed continued to stay with her as a companion and showed her a river of water of life in front of the throne. It sparkled like crystal. It looked like a sea of glass, "flowing" from the throne of God down the middle of the city's street. On each side of the river was the Tree of Life.[6]

Surrounding the throne were four living creatures who sang nonstop: "Holy, holy, holy, is the Lord God Almighty, who was, who is, and who is to come."[7] She continued to hear voices singing and worshiping. As she listened more closely these immortal words filled her ears:

> *You are worthy, our Lord and God, to receive glory and honor and power, For you created all things, and by your will they were created and have their being.* Revelation 4:11, NIV

Suzanne was in such awe of all this that she became caught up in the worship of the One who was sitting on the throne. Just as natural as taking a breath, she too began to praise God the Father, *her* Lord and *her* God.

Suzanne then turned toward the crystal-clear river and looked to see where it was going; it was a color she had never seen before. The colors were new and exciting! There were layers of beauty. The river wound down and looped around and on each side, she noticed there were throngs of people. As she observed these people, they began approaching her, and she perceived that she knew them and they knew her![8] Straightaway, she recognized her mother, smiling and holding her arms out to Suzanne. She then saw her grandparents; all four of them and they too were smiling and laughing while gesturing and waving at her. Suzanne became so excited. She saw other family members and friends, and they all began to excitedly approach her. She'd known them all before, and she knew them all as believers in Christ. Each individual possessed distinguishing characteristics. Suzanne felt like she was being welcomed to a party that only she was exclusively invited to. There was so much excitement that surrounded her arrival here. The laughter and joy were contagious. She felt a thrill as she gazed upon each one of their faces. She was received by all who were present here. It was as though a table had been recently set with a place designated just for her and everyone here was waiting for her arrival. She had no thought about anything earthly or what she'd left behind; instead, she thought to herself, *I'm home* and at the same time, she sensed her new life here would have a very real purpose, so different from the one she'd left behind. Mostly, the feeling of excitement she was now experiencing was from the knowledge that she had overcome.

Thoughts she'd previously had upon leaving her body as she traveled through the massive universe of feeling so small and insignificant in a creation that was infinite and vast was quickly exchanged for a new thought and a new truth: She was *precious and valuable, and she belonged.* Suzanne was created by God, and her home was here with Him—*He wanted her here.* This was her divine appointment after having completed a journey on earth and everything about this new life was peace and perfection. She was in a place unlike any other place that she could have ever imagined. She was seeing, hearing and understanding things on a new level and a new dimension that she never knew nor understood.

Suzanne marveled at the realization that she was here, and she was excited to explore her new surroundings. Everything that was unknown would now be known because she would experience it for herself. There were so many more dimensions here.

The colors were unlike anything she'd ever seen before and there were so many more here than on earth. As the light swept over them, they had an energy and vivacity that made her feel as though they were interacting with her. There were different facets and layers to each color and they exuded so many different shades and levels of clarity and there was life in each color! It was as though they danced before her. The beauty and the light surrounded her.

As Suzanne continued taking in and processing her new environment, she examined her surroundings; there were waterfalls and streams and lakes, all active and interacting with her. She was enveloped by beautiful bodies of water all with their own unique and distinguishable plant life.

On the horizon, she saw different landscapes—mountains, hills, forests and deserts as well as lakes, rivers and streams. Each of these different landscapes were in an untouched, virginal state of beauty and each contained flowers, plants, trees, animals, birds and insects; each one for that particular landscape and they were all flawless and incorruptible. Their beauty was at their peak of loveliness.

All of God's creation operated and functioned together in perfect harmony like a grand symphony on a grand stage. They each performed with purpose and simultaneously worked together to worship God, their Creator in their magnificent splendor. Everything cooperated and functioned without any earthly complications such as heat or cold, disease or decay. It was astonishing and arresting at first sight. They were each one in unison, one with another. Suzanne had the knowledge that creation was set free from its curse and was performing on this heavenly stage for its Creator as well as all the inhabitants here.

She saw creation as intended by God. The trees were at their optimum state of beauty, perfect with nothing dead or dying in their midst; the grass had the most beautiful hues of green with no weeds hampering its performance; each blade was without a single flaw. The flowers stood erect and each bloom was at its peak of beauty. Every type of flower ever created flaunted itself here and stood blooming in beautiful colors; some she had never seen.

The water held distinct shades of blue, yet it was crystal clear with nothing to limit its attractiveness like bacteria or algae. It sparkled like thousands of diamonds and glistened beyond comprehension because the light came from everywhere—the light came from Jesus.

This passage of Scripture instantly came to mind:

Against its will, all creation was subjected to God's curse. But with eager hope, the creation looks forward to the day when it will join God's children in glorious freedom from death and decay. For we know that all creation has been groaning as in the pains of childbirth right up to the present time. Romans 8:20-22

She realized that because Jesus was here and alive, the Word was active and alive because the Word became flesh and was here with her. She was knowledgeable of all Scripture because it dwelt here and was completely accessible to her and she had the full mind of Christ.

Everything here was new; everything old, including her sick body, had passed away.[9] And just as this Scripture was being revealed to her, she glanced down at herself realizing she now possessed a new body—a very beautiful body without a single flaw; it wasn't old, sick or capable of sin or susceptible to death.

Again, she simply held this knowledge without being told. She was in awe of herself and elated beyond belief, yet she felt no pride within herself. She was now inhabiting a beautiful *heavenly body* and she was clothed in white.[10] Yet, she knew that she still looked just like herself.[11]

> *And there are heavenly bodies and earthly bodies; the beauty that belongs to heavenly bodies is different from the beauty that belongs to earthly bodies. The sun has its own beauty, the moon another beauty, and the stars a different beauty; and even among stars there are different kinds of beauty. This is how it will be when the dead are raised to life. When the body is buried, it is mortal; when raised, it will be immortal. When buried, it is ugly and weak; when raised, it will be beautiful and strong. When buried, it is a physical body; when raised, it will be a spiritual body. There is, of course, a physical body, so there has to be a spiritual body.*
> 1 Corinthians 15:40-44, GNT

As she continued to witness all of these new insights and explore and discover all of these truths, while at the same time experiencing the praises going forth to the throne of God, she felt overcome by the astounding beauty of it all. Very solemnly and reverently, Suzanne lifted her face up toward the light, and she knew she was in the very presence of Jesus. She fell to her knees in humble adoration of Him. Light and love penetrated out from Him to her. And she knew within herself that she was known and loved by Him. It was old knowledge and new knowledge; it was ageless and timeless.

Jesus gazed upon her knowingly with a love that washed over her like a huge wave. Jesus knew her, and she knew Him … it was like the intimacy between lovers. She was so aware of the huge price He paid for her to enter this miraculous kingdom. Suzanne witnessed His nail-scarred hands and feet, gratitude overwhelmed her as she realized more intensely than ever before exactly what Jesus sacrificed for her. She was overcome with a sincere thankfulness and love toward Him; for His willingness to die for her. She clearly saw God's love for her that sent His only son, Jesus, to be the perfect and only acceptable sacrifice for her. This love from God her Father was an endless love from ages past that flooded her very being. She knew she was not here by her own merit, not by anything she did, but only by what she believed. She was lost and cut off from God by her sin, but Christ died for her and when she accepted and believed the simple truth of that message, she knew clearly that her faith in Him and Him alone was the only way she was able to be here now. And again, this Scripture came to her mind.

> *No one can come to me unless the Father who sent me draws them, and I will raise them up at the last day.* John 6:44

She saw how Jesus was her High Priest and He gave her the ability to approach God through Him. And once she received Jesus, He sat at the right hand of God interceding for her day and night as her very own High Priest. There was no curtain or anything else to separate her from Father God. Jesus was the bridge that closed the gap between her and God. Her acceptance of Jesus' death and resurrection gave her the right to be here.

She was aware that the Holy Spirit of God was the one who pursued her on earth and prompted her to believe while she was still in bondage to her humanity. The Holy Spirit courted her like a lover and wooed her to come to God through Christ; He never stopped His pursuit of her right up to the moment of her acceptance of Jesus. And each moment after, He'd guided her and helped her to grow in her faith.

All this knowledge was now impressed upon her. This was a truth that each one of Heaven's inhabitants understood.

God the Father received her unto Himself because of her faith in these things—the knowledge of her sin, the sorrow for her sin and her belief and acceptance of Christ's blood for her sin. This reconciliation was free to her by faith in this profound truth.

God the Father, Jesus the Son and the Holy Spirit were three Divine Beings, yet they were inseparably one. They simply were and had always been. They were the Alpha and the Omega; the first and the last; the beginning and the end. Their goal was always to love, woo and reconcile all creation to them. Suzanne was reconciled to God through Christ's blood. She was now here in the place that was prepared for her.

Knowledge was all around her revealing more and more truth to her. Then her companion, her angel, presented her to Jesus as though presenting a trophy knowing that Jesus was the one who made the true sacrifice. Her angel had been assigned to help protect her on earth and carry out the will of the Father. Jesus was aware of all his efforts to help Suzanne. And then the angelic being bid Suzanne goodbye because he was being given a new assignment.

Suzanne continued to hear astonishing and remarkable sounds and voices all around her; thousands upon thousands of angelic and non-angelic voices singing Glory to God and praising His Name while beautiful angelic beings played musical instruments. It was mystifying and arresting and undeniably the most breathtaking experience she'd ever seen or heard. The songs and praises she heard continued to reveal the same truth to each one of the inhabitants here. Truth was being told through the voices, the music and even the beauty. The creation and the voices as well as the colors and the beauty continued to praise God and the Lamb of God who alone was worthy as the Spirit inspired this heavenly music and all the beauty that was here.

The praises to God and to the Lamb of God were the very breath of Heaven. Her new home would be an experience to explore for ages and ages to come. Suzanne was aware that there was a plan and purpose for her here in Heaven also. There were multitudes of people all around her, each with their own identity, purpose and destiny. She knew that their pleasure and her pleasure was in praising God the Father and Jesus, His Son, while at the same time there was a thrill and an excitement of what their unique purpose would be in Heaven.

Each person belonged here just as she did and every inch of creation possessed a distinct plan they would each one carry out. As she stood and pondered the magnitude of it all, she glanced up and there stood a girl in her twenties ... *a very familiar girl.*

CHAPTER 5

Loss and Grieving

*The Lord is close to the brokenhearted
and saves those who are crushed in spirit.*
Psalms 34:18, NIV

Suzanne
1991 and 1992

Suzanne could not function. The evening her husband, Paul died, they were just two weeks away from celebrating their seventeenth wedding anniversary, and the very next day after that she would have celebrated her fortieth birthday. Their daughter and only child, Erin, was just fourteen when she lost her father.

After Paul's accident, Suzanne and Erin struggled separately. Suzanne was not capable of helping her daughter mourn her father because her own pain was so overwhelming that it literally paralyzed her ability to move forward. She couldn't dig herself out of her own grief-stricken nightmare long enough to begin to comfort Erin, nor did she seek help for either of them. So, they both struggled alone for months, surviving as best they could—each one subconsciously choosing a different method to heal their broken hearts with neither of their choices having any power to soothe or mend their sorrow.

Suzanne withdrew at first and slept a lot. She no longer cleaned the house, she stopped showering on a daily basis, and she stopped dressing in her trendy outfits as she once had; instead she wore sweats and T-shirts or just remained in her pajamas all day. She abandoned the kitchen and quit making her once healthy and nutritionally balanced meals. She withdrew from talking with her friends. She was depressed. If anyone could have helped her, she would have rejected it. She chose to remain in her sadness; she would not even try to heal, because she loved Paul and Paul was gone; *So really,* she thought, *what was the point?*

Realistically and on a psychological level, Suzanne knew she needed to get on with her life but she was powerless to do so. Paul died in mid-June and it was now September.

She and Erin barely made it through the summer. It went by quickly and seemed like one big blur to her. Suzanne felt and looked ten years older. Erin went away with a new friend, Christy, to the beach in July for a week. The family tried to be helpful and invited Suzanne as well but, of course, she declined and urged Erin to go without her. Suzanne felt a lot of guilt about that but, unfortunately, guilt was not enough to motivate her to change any of the choices she made or was now making.

While her daughter was away, she'd spent hours

on the sofa with no desire to do anything and she cried a lot. The days sped by while she did nothing productive. She slept intermittently throughout the day leaving the television on for noise but watching nothing in particular.

And then that depressing summer ended and fall arrived like an unwelcome solicitor standing on her threshold knocking on her door hoping to be welcomed, but Suzanne was not interested.

Erin turned fifteen on September 2nd. Thankfully, a long-time friend of their family invited both of them to the beach for Labor Day weekend but Suzanne wearily declined the invitation making the excuse that she "just needed some more time." Yet, again, she urged Erin to go. That Labor Day weekend fell on Erin's birthday and Suzanne felt like the world's worst mom, but even then, she hadn't changed her mind. She gave Erin money and told her to buy something special, something she'd always wanted. But what Erin wanted, money could not buy. Suzanne wanted to care—*but her heart wasn't into doing life anymore.* She knew she was letting Erin down, and she knew others thought so too, but she just couldn't pull herself together.

Paul's death caused Suzanne to stop parenting her daughter. Suzanne knew this but she did nothing to change it. She was relieved when school started back up and Erin began to ride to school with the friend she'd gone to the beach with. Christy and her mother would stop by the house and pick Erin up each morning. She knew this family also went to the same church they attended the few short months before Paul's accident. Catherine seemed nice and Suzanne knew she meant well. But when she'd tried to strike up a conversation with Suzanne, too many times, Suzanne withdrew into her shell. Catherine was one of those women who had it all together. She still had her husband and family. There was probably a little white picket fence around her house and most likely she baked cookies every day and owned a little white dog. No, she was not going to open up to this woman and talk about how she felt. She could not. Suzanne used to be just like her; she knew exactly how her perfect little life was. She knew Erin was spending a lot of time with this woman and her daughter, but wasn't that okay? Suzanne was certain that she could not be what Erin needed right now, so couldn't she at least let the perfect little church lady do it for her? Suzanne knew she was wrong in all of her assumptions, she knew her attitude was so off—and normally, this lady was just the type of friend she would want. They met back in the spring and she truly liked her and was looking forward to getting to know her. So … she wondered to herself, *why was she judging her so harshly now? What was wrong with trying to be a good neighbor?*

Suzanne would muddle through her day. She would pilfer through the mail and pay the bills but she didn't have any clear direction. Sometimes she would head out to the patio and sit in one of the new chairs that she and Paul purchased when they moved into their new home. She would think about Paul and how she never would have imagined that *this* is how her life would have ended up. She was still in shock.

The worst and most depressing thing she did was to get out their photo albums when Erin was away. She would become lost in her thoughts as she turned page after page wishing for the past. She would cry and beg God to let it all just be a bad dream. She would ask Him why things couldn't just go back to the way they were. Then she would become so angry at God because she knew that this is how it really was and nothing was going to change it. Sometimes she would see evidence that Erin had been looking at them too because photos were missing of Paul and Erin together and the mom inside her would ache for Erin. Why couldn't they do this together? Grief was such a robber. She was so confused about God and His goodness.

In the afternoon, when Erin came home, she would suggest she microwave a frozen dinner, eat a sandwich or fix a bowl of cereal. Sometimes, she might drive Erin to a fast food restaurant for a burger or offer to get some Chinese takeout or have a pizza delivered. When they were in the car together, they never talked much about anything, at least nothing of any importance. Suzanne and Erin rarely made eye contact with one another and neither of them could come up with anything to say to each other anymore. Suzanne made trips to the grocery store at odd hours of the night. She knew she was failing her daughter and that Erin was in pain as well. Yet, Erin went to school and *that was a positive thing, wasn't it?* She still spent time with friends and seemed to be functioning okay, at least that is what Suzanne wanted to believe. She still looked alright to her. She'd bought Erin lots of new clothes over the summer before Paul died and Erin was still wearing all those cute outfits which she knew only covered her exterior, the pain on the inside was screaming for attention.

Erin was so different now, just like she was different. Everything changed between the two of them. They interacted differently now and it was hard for them to communicate. Suzanne knew she needed to see a doctor or a counselor, but she couldn't seem to drag herself away from this overwhelming grief and endless pain. She wanted to get back to a routine of cooking, cleaning and doing laundry. She so wanted to see normal again but she did not know what that looked like and thought, *She was going to need a job too,* but there that part of her that didn't care anymore.

She was secretly pleased when Erin began doing her own laundry and some of the housecleaning. Suzanne wondered all the time *Where was God that night?* She would cry and blame God for everything. The one thought that took precedence over all her other thoughts was that *God could have protected Paul from the accident* and that single thought took her further down her road of hopelessness.

Suzanne came to Christ when she was a senior in high school. She watched a Billy Graham crusade that took place in New York City and was televised live. She remembered the date, it was October 5th, 1969. Back then, she was preparing to leave home for the first time in her life. She was headed to college and was so very excited about her future. She could not have been more ready to leave home. Her father was an alcoholic ever since she could remember. He was getting worse every day, and she could not wait to get away from him. She loved her mother and they were close; she felt sorry for her mom *but she needed to get out of that house.*

One night, she was ironing some clothes while watching TV. The evangelist, Reverend Graham, was preaching on the Second Coming of Christ. It was a message she never heard, and she realized she was not saved and would go to hell if she were to die or if Jesus were to return. He talked about Jesus coming back "as a thief in the night"—unexpectedly and in the twinkling of an eye—and those words interested and scared her at the same time. She wanted to be prepared. She listened intently to the North Carolina evangelist as he shared the message telling people to come just as they are and to make a decision in their heart to accept Christ for what He had done for them. At the close of his sermon when the altar call was given, Suzanne accepted Christ. She remembered the choir singing "Just As I Am" as her eyes shone with tears. At that very moment, she understood that Jesus was God's Son, and she accepted His death on the cross as payment for her sins. She would never forget the minute her life changed. She even wrote in for some material and upon receiving it, she read it all and, once she'd gone off to college, she found a place to worship with some other students. But, Suzanne had never encountered a true crisis.

She met Paul during her third year of college; he was a year ahead of her and was majoring in Business. Suzanne wanted to be a teacher and was majoring in Education. After Paul graduated, he began working and they continued dating while she finished college and went on to teach school. They married one year after she graduated from college in May of 1974, which was one day before her birthday. She wanted to finish her teaching position and still have a June wedding. Her mom joked that her wedding was her birthday present that year. No matter how much she wished her dad would have been a real father to her that day, he stumbled as he escorted her down the aisle and slurred his words while everyone simply overlooked his behavior as always.

Suzanne continued to teach school until Erin was born two years later on September 2, 1976. Things were good between she and Paul and they were a happy couple. Paul was a newcomer in the business of managing commercial real estate so he wasn't making a whole lot of money. However, when Erin was born, they both agreed that Suzanne would be a stay-at-home mom because they wanted more children; strangely, Suzanne never conceived again. Even though finances were tight, Suzanne still enjoyed being a new mother. So, for the first few years, they watched every penny. Suzanne settled into parenting their daughter. Her goal was to be an exceptional wife and mother. She volunteered at church and at Erin's school. Because of her background in education, she even substituted sometimes for extra money. Mostly, she loved experimenting with cooking and gardening. She planned vacations when they could afford it and enjoyed their simple life. It seemed to her that things were going better than she could have hoped.

Church was always more important to Suzanne than for Paul, but she figured most men were like that. She did not have another man to compare him to because of her father's minimal participation in her life. Paul was a dream compared to her more often than not intoxicated dad. She realized Paul was busy and carried a lot on his mind. He went to church with her, yet she never heard him talk about God, and somehow, she did not think he felt the same way about God as she did. They never prayed together and she wished for that.

Once, while they were still dating, Suzanne shared with Paul her salvation experience. He seemed happy for her, but he did not share anything back with her or tell her about a decisive moment in his own life. He did voice to her that day that he believed in God, yet Jesus was never mentioned. Suzanne didn't question it anymore. Later, after they were married, she would ponder that conversation from time to time and wonder about his eternal security. Whenever she brought it up to him, he would become agitated at her probing him. She knew faith was a personal thing, so she hadn't pressed. Paul was such a great husband to her and a superb father to Erin. She felt when she married Paul she won the jackpot compared to her own father and watching how miserable her mother's life was through the years. What more could she ask for?

The years passed and Erin entered middle school and then high school. Soon, they could finally afford a nicer home. So just that past January, they moved to a new area of town, a home they were all excited about. It was a nice step up for them and with all the excitement of moving and making selections for their new home, Suzanne did not have a chance to become acquainted with the neighbors or make friends at their new church. She planned to, but then just a few months later, everything slid out from under them.

Regardless of the lack of close relationships, some of the women in the church, including Catherine, whom she met earlier that summer, brought food and left sympathy cards after Paul's death. Friends from their previous church and a few of Paul's business associates sent things too. She froze some of the food and it lasted for over a month, especially since she and Erin ate so little. When all those dishes and casseroles were depleted, she was forced out of her self-made emotional prison to leave the house and replenish. She used to be so healthy and couldn't believe how she was compromising her nutritional standards so quickly, but she just didn't care anymore. God had let her down. Paul lost his life and he took her life and her future with him. She knew she should care. She knew she needed to be there for Erin, but she couldn't. She was very aware that her relationship with Erin was nothing like it used to be. Erin was always closer to her father. Suzanne knew she missed him desperately. She wished she could fix things for her; she couldn't even fix things for herself. She did not know how to get out of this pain or how to get rid of this unending sadness. Suzanne knew Erin was spending time with people she didn't know and spending a lot of time at school and the library. She thought that was positive for her. She felt Erin was actually better off with strangers than with her. Suzanne knew she needed to cook and clean and just *go get a haircut*. She needed to get out of the house, but she simply didn't have the desire or the energy.

Most days, she still could not believe that Paul was gone. It all happened so quickly. She and Erin were simply waiting for Paul to come home from work so they could fulfill their Friday night tradition of eating out together. Instead, a drunk driver heading down the wrong side of the road changed everything that night for all of them. That was that; it wouldn't change. Her life and Erin's life was turned upside down the moment she received the call from the highway patrol to come to the hospital. It felt to her that her life had shattered like glass in a million pieces right in front of her, and she was left to put them all back together, alone. That is exactly how she saw things.

Suzanne did not feel God's presence anymore. Her faith was shaken, and she wondered why God would abandon her. She just could not understand how a loving God could allow this to happen. She truly trusted Him all of these years since that night she invited Christ in her life; she truly believed in Him. But now? She just didn't know anymore. She would think, *Is this what happens to Christians?* While the pieces of her life remained scattered, waiting to be put back together, she didn't know how or where to begin to pick up the first piece.

A crisis *had happened*, and now Suzanne needed to figure out what to do and how to handle it. She needed to decide whether or not she still believed in God—and if she did, how would she allow her faith to walk her through this uncharted territory?

Right now, she knew nothing at all about any of that and, in all honesty, she did not know how she would begin to take the first step. She wondered, *What would that even look like?*

CHAPTER 6

The Procedure

*I do not understand what I do.
For what I want to do I do not do,
but what I hate I do.*

Romans 7:15, NIV

Erin

Wednesday, January 15, 1992

"Ashley," the voice called again and Erin realized it was the name she gave the lady at the front desk when she paid her money as well as the name on the ID card. Hearing it startled her, but quickly, she twisted her head around toward the voice and made eye contact with the woman holding the door open with her backside. "We're ready for you," she said. Erin stood, took a shaky, shallow breath and gathered her book bag and coat and walked toward the woman as she stood with her sunny smile by the entrance holding a clipboard. "Come right this way," she said.

The woman escorted Erin down a hallway, and as they turned corners and passed by several closed doors, they ended up in what looked to be a regular examination room. Erin was shown inside and then instructed by this woman to sit on the exam table that was positioned in the middle of the room. There were metal things sticking out of the sides and Erin, having never been to a gynecologist, didn't even know what they were called or their purpose. She obediently stepped up on the platform, turned and sat down on the exam table and faced the woman. The woman then said, "Based upon your last period, it looks like you are about ten weeks along?" Erin nodded and muttered, "I guess so." The woman then handed Erin a gown and said very matter-of-factly, "Remove all of your clothes including your panties and bra and put this gown on with the opening in the back." The woman held out a bag and said, "Put all your clothes, your handbag and any other loose items in this plastic bag. It will be waiting for you in the recovery room where you will go when you are finished. Do you have any questions?" Erin shook her head no and said, "Ummm … no, I don't think so." Erin noticed the name written across the front of the bag was not her name, instead, it read "Ashley Brown." Then the woman added before exiting the room, "The nurse will be right in." After she was gone, Erin began to undress and put the gown on she was given. She noticed some droplets of dried blood on the floor and felt a little uneasy. She finished tying the gown in the back and proceeded to fold her clothes and stuff them in the bag on top of her book bag, which she placed at the very bottom for security; she then laid her coat next to it, because it would not fit in the bag. She cinched the bag and placed it and her coat on the floor while realizing that inside held all the things that belonged to a girl who did not belong in a place such as this. Then, she did just as she was told and obediently sat herself up on the crinkly white paper in the oversized cotton gown and waited, hands folded in her lap as the minutes melted away.

Soon, another woman came in the room—a nurse she assumed because of her matching scrubs. She instructed Erin to lie back and place her feet in the strange metals things they called "stirrups." Erin reluctantly obeyed while still trying to keep her legs together. Moments later, a doctor came charging through the door as if he were in a huge hurry and without even stopping to introduce himself or pause to make eye contact with Erin, he began talking with the nurse. Erin did not think he acted like any doctor she ever met on past visits to the pediatrician with her mom or for that matter, any of the doctors they met that night her dad died.

He sat down on the little round metal rolling stool that was positioned in front of the exam table. He pulled on an elastic glove and told her to open her legs wider. Erin had already placed her feet in the stirrups but she was so embarrassed. She reluctantly opened her legs wider but the nurse leaned over and pushed them apart some more. She locked eyes with Erin and held her gaze; she then very sternly stated, "You'll need to relax." Erin thought to herself, *How in the world will I ever do that?* The doctor then proceeded to examine Erin. He told her to relax and inserted his fingers inside her while pushing down on her abdomen with his other hand. It hurt and Erin squirmed a little. The nurse remained beside Erin continuing to give orders while restraining her by leaning over her a bit, "Relax," she breathed in a low voice and Erin could smell the coffee on her breath. She then informed the doctor that Erin was ten weeks along and he nodded in agreement. While all of this was happening, another nurse came in with a syringe and a bottle of liquid. She handed it to the doctor and left the room. When Erin tried to raise her head off the table to observe what was going on, the nurse snapped at her once again in an unsympathetic tone of voice ordering her to, "Lie back … just relax."

Erin was scared, and she tried to pull away. She began to tremble a little. The nurse told her she would have to calm down and this would be over soon. She then instructed her to spread her legs very wide. Still sitting on the stool, the doctor twisted around and began to fill a syringe with the contents of the bottle.

The nurse proceeded to tell her he was dispensing some numbing medicine and it would help with the pain. He then turned back towards her, finally making eye contact with Erin and said directly to her, "Lie very still, this will burn a little." Then he proceeded to insert the needle into her cervix. Erin felt a prick down there as well as a burning sensation. She was terrified now; what had she done? What on earth was she doing?

The doctor then rose and walked out of the room. The nurse standing by the table spoke to Erin again and said in a distant way, "Honey, the sooner you can relax, the sooner this will be over, it won't take more than just a few more minutes." Then she too left and when she closed the door behind her, Erin was left all alone in this inhospitable, barren room.

Erin became afraid. She pulled her legs out of the stirrups. She bent her knees and pulled them up close to her while wrapping her arms around herself and lacing her fingers together and then proceeded to lean over herself. She felt so helpless and began to cry. Why was she here? She wished she could have talked to someone. She was in a mess. She wanted her mom, and she missed her daddy. How could Michael have done this to her? Why didn't he care about her? She didn't want to be here. She then tried to calm herself wIth a thought about leaving but when she looked around the room for her clothes, they were already gone. One of the nurses who was in the room must have taken the bag out along with her coat. Erin was so scared and distracted that she did not even notice.

In a few minutes, the hateful nurse opened the door and came in with the doctor. They were laughing about something, and again, the doctor didn't even acknowledge Erin. She felt like a non-person. She wondered why he wouldn't look at her or meet her eyes or even acknowledge her existence. Another nurse followed behind them wheeling in a laboratory looking machine with a funny hose attached to what looked to be two glass containers. When that nurse exited the room, she shut the door behind her and Erin's heart leapt within her chest. The doctor again sat down on the little round rolling stool and positioned himself once more; he seemed to be in a hurry to get this over with. The nurse, noticing Erin's position, began barking orders once again, "Put your feet back in the stirrups," which Erin immediately did, this time without a second thought. The nurse then covered the lower portion of Erin's body with a sheet and the doctor placed one of his hands on her inner thigh, picked up the funny hose and instructed her to "be very still."

Soon, Erin felt a foreign object being inserted inside her. The nurse leaned over and flipped a switch on the machine. She heard a low hum that sounded a little bit like a vacuum cleaner. Erin felt a lot of pressure and some tugging—a lot of weird noises— gurgling, squirting and sucking sounds filled her ears. The nurse continued to monitor Erin very closely as she leaned over her a bit prepared to restrain her if necessary. She locked eyes with Erin daring her to react or move or cause one single problem for the doctor. She very quietly whispered to Erin, "Moving will create problems for the doctor and you too, so lie as still as possible, this will be over in just a couple of minutes."

Erin was terrified and just kept whispering, "Okay, okay." She heard the nurse and doctor talking, she didn't understand their medical jargon but soon, the nurse reached over and flipped the machine off. It was as if Erin was not even there. The doctor removed the thing he put inside her. He then studied what was in the machine for a few seconds, he said something about number one being extracted and intact and the nurse nodded in agreement. He then placed the hose back in its position near the machine. He rose from the stool and walked out of the room without even speaking to Erin. The second nurse came in again and wheeled the machine out. Erin realized all this time she was staring at the clock on the wall and when it was over, it read 1:32 p.m. The strange thought occurred to her that if she were not here, she would be in American History right about now. The nurse who'd been in the room with her all along proceeded to fasten a sanitary belt around her hips and secure a Kotex to it while positioning it between her legs. All the while, Erin was feeling dizzy and queasy.

The nurse then instructed Erin to take her feet out of the stirrups. She offered her a hand to help her off the table. Erin did as she was instructed, but upon rising, she felt weak and began to shake. The nurse simply told her to follow her. Erin rose and looked down at the exam table where she was lying and when she saw the blood, she felt like she might pass out. Yet, she proceeded to follow the nurse down the hall to another room which consisted of several cots; there were rows and rows of them.

The room was hushed and gloomy, the shades were drawn and the lights were turned down low and it took Erin's eyes a few seconds to adjust. The nurse escorted her over to an empty cot, she saw the bag with the fake name on it containing her clothing and her coat was beside it. It was such a comfort to see her clothes and know that she would soon be out of here. It was hard for Erin to see well, but there were several girls lying down on the cots. Some of the beds were empty except for crumpled up blankets, looking as though someone just crawled out of them. She noticed one girl was crying softly and another girl was just simply staring into the darkness; others looked as though they might be sleeping. The nurse instructed her to lie down and rest awhile. She was told they would let her know when she could leave. Erin lay down but she was shaking and cold and the nurse unfolded a blanket and spread it over her saying, "It is normal to be cold, this will help." She then simply walked away. A few minutes later, a lady came in and offered her some seven-up and Tylenol.

Erin cried softly and her entire body shook while she lay in the darkness before finally falling asleep. Two hours later, she woke up abruptly when she heard a voice saying, "We're swamped with walk-in's and we don't have enough beds, can you clear some out of recovery?"

Soon, a nurse came in and took her temperature. "Okay," she said, "You can go, here is a sheet of paper for you to read, follow the instructions. Your clothes are right here in the bag beside your bed. You can change across the hall when it's free and then leave through the back door. You'll see the exit sign in the back. Make sure you go out that way."

Erin sat up and took the paper from her, locating once more the plastic bag containing her things. She watched as the nurse walked over to another girl and took her temperature. Erin then removed the covers and stood up. When she stood, she felt empty and drained and tired. She reached down and picked up the bag along with her coat and walked across the hall to the area the woman pointed her to. There was a long curtain pulled back for privacy and Erin realized someone was inside dressing, so she waited.

Soon, a young girl with long brown hair came out of the dressing room. Erin thought she was so pretty. She recognized her from school; she was a year ahead of her, a cheerleader and one of the *popular* girls. She wore makeup and pretty pink lipstick and she was wearing cool clothes. She wasn't smiling but she seemed just fine to Erin. She couldn't believe she just had an abortion—*based on how she looked*. The girl met Erin's eyes for just a moment, then slung her purse over her shoulder and said, "I'm done, you can go in now." Erin thanked her and then she entered through the opening and pulled the curtain together to begin her own transformation.

She noticed a half-empty box of Kotex. Erin realized she was bleeding very heavily now, so she grabbed a couple of the napkins out of the box and stuffed them in her book bag. She then removed the soiled one she was wearing and placed it in the nearby trash can and replaced it with a fresh one.

She was still feeling a bit shaky when she removed the gown and began to rummage through the bag that contained her things. She felt so dirty and when she removed the gown, she saw that she had bled all over it. She quickly stuffed it in a hamper that read, "Dirty Gowns."

Erin dressed, stood up, looked in the mirror and then she ran her fingers through her long blonde hair to smooth it out a little. She picked up her coat and book bag, pulled the curtain back and walked out of the dressing room. Another girl stood waiting.

Erin saw the exit sign the woman pointed out to

her and walked out of the clinic into the crisp, cold January air. She felt empty and sad. She knew that she walked out a totally different girl than she was when she stepped into that place.

Erin began to carefully walk along the sidewalk, it was cold out but the sun was bright and warmed her face as she squinted in the afternoon sun; everything felt so different. Her stomach hurt severely. It felt like menstrual cramps but worse than anything she'd ever experienced.

She slowly and carefully strolled back to the bus stop to wait for the next bus to arrive. The crowd of people standing around were talking and laughing with one another. Erin wanted to yell at them to stop. But instead, she just stood there and waited for the bus to come and when it did, she hurried on to find a seat where she could sit by herself. Erin sat staring out of the window the rest of the way thinking about absolutely nothing as the bus ambled down the road, stopping and starting as strangers entered and exited the bus that had taken her to a place that changed her from a girl to a grown up. Not only that, but her heart was different too; her heart was now encased in emotional pain that would take years to unlock and find freedom from. She needed to take one more bus to get home, but soon she was back in her neighborhood among familiar surroundings.

When she arrived home that day, her mom was up and even showered—*which was a miracle*. She asked Erin how school was. "Fine," Erin answered her, "but I don't feel well; I got my period today and I have bad cramps." She added nonchalantly, "If the school calls, I spent most of the day in the bathroom with cramps; I was sick." She then went to the kitchen, retrieved a glass from the dishwasher and filled it up with tap water. She grabbed a bottle of Tylenol from the medicine cabinet and went to bed. Erin lay there all night in her bed, crying and bleeding and thinking about her baby. She hugged her white bear and she thought about her daddy. She blocked Michael out of her mind.

Her mom never came in to check on her. She woke up the next morning and went to school as if nothing ever happened.

CHAPTER 7

Starting Over

Carry each other's burdens,
and in this way you will
fulfill the law of Christ.
Galatians 6:2, NIV

Suzanne and Catherine
January, 1992

Catherine continued calling Suzanne. She called once a week after Paul died, and when the summer was over and school started, she would call a couple of times a month. Suzanne would always listen patiently to her predictable questions answering each one of them as politely as possible usually mumbling something in reply like, "Yes, she was getting by, and no, she didn't need anything." Then she would thank her for her call. When she hung up the phone, she felt this woman's phone calls were pointless. She was glad she succeeded in pulling away once again. *She barely knew this lady*. Their daughters were friends, and she was grateful she was helping her by giving Erin rides to school. She was painfully aware that they went to the same church—*back when Suzanne actually went to church*.

But today, when Catherine showed up to drive Erin to school, she gently tapped on the door and asked Suzanne if she could come back and have a cup of coffee with her, "My treat," she said. Surprisingly, Suzanne agreed to her offer. The offer came when Suzanne was finally desperate for help, as well as friendship. It was approximately six months since Paul's death, and she must *get it together*.

After Erin left with Catherine and Christy for school, Suzanne showered and dressed. She didn't feel like she owned one piece of clothing that looked right to her anymore. She'd lost a lot of weight and her hair needed cutting and styling. She could also use some color or highlights; anything would help.

She had been so mad at God for so long. Just that week though, she was trying to read her Bible and prayed and asked Him to help her—*If He was at all capable*—she thought sarcastically. She was still so cynical and a bit mocking toward God. She honestly didn't know if she could ever trust Him again. Although, she hoped somehow, she could make it back to Him. Deep down, it was what she wanted and somewhere in the recesses of her mind, she knew her faith in Christ was her only answer. She began to dialog with God while still rooted in anger. Suzanne was honest, and she'd reluctantly begun to talk to God about her pain. She picked her Bible up just this week and read a Scripture that she bookmarked a couple of years ago: *"For I know the plans I have for you, plans to prosper you and not to harm you, plans to give you hope and a future"* (Jeremiah 29:11, NIV). And her heart leapt within her. And then she simply questioned whether the Bible was full of lies. Inwardly, she knew she believed the truth of this passage, but why all of this? Good plans? Paul's death? A hope and a future? What does that even mean? Where was God? Then Suzanne began to sob uncontrollably as her shoulders shook with despair. She tried to calm herself and, in an attempt to connect with her Lord, she lifted her eyes up to the ceiling and simply cried out to the God she knew *before the accident*. Suzanne prayed an honest prayer and asked Jesus to please help her. That was two days ago; she was now dressing to meet a woman she barely knew.

Catherine arrived back at Suzanne's house around nine and gently tapped on the door. She carried a couple of take-out coffees from McDonald's, she brought cream and sugar and napkins and little plastic stir sticks because she didn't know how Suzanne liked her coffee. They sat and talked until around eleven. Suzanne shared her thoughts and feelings and talked out her frustration about her faith and her doubts about God. She talked a lot about Paul and how much she missed him. Catherine mostly listened and when it seemed that Suzanne still needed to talk, she offered to take her out to lunch to a little place not far from here and, surprisingly to them both, Suzanne agreed.

Catherine was an attractive woman in her late thirties with short, wavy, black hair and cropped bangs. Her eyes were hazel and her skin was fair. Her face was round, and she wore a little makeup but mostly, her look was natural. Her lips were very full and she accented them with gloss. She dressed in a pair of dark blue jeans and wore an oversized, olive green sweater that brought out the green in her eyes. She wore brown leather boots and added a pair of dangly earrings to her outfit. She seemed stylish to Suzanne and looked like she kept up with the current fashion trends; it seemed she had it all together and Suzanne was somewhat intimidated by her. But Catherine possessed an inner beauty and confidence and Suzanne was wise enough to know where it came from.

When Suzanne dressed earlier that morning while waiting for Catherine to return from taking the girls to school and bring the coffee back, she pulled out some faded jeans that were now baggy, she then grabbed a button down, white oxford style shirt with several vertical pleats in it. She put on a pair of ballerina flats and ran a comb through her hair. She had lost a lot of her hair back in the summer. It came out in clumps from all the stress within weeks of Paul's death. When she studied herself in the mirror, she saw a woman that looked very tired. Her auburn brown hair was medium in length and in desperate need of a good haircut. She wore no bangs; the only thing she could do was pull it up. Her eyes were dark brown. Her cheek bones were high but looked hollowed out now from all the weight she'd lost. Her skin was ivory with some blotchy red patches so she used some foundation and a little powder to even it out. She applied a little bit of mascara along with some neutral eye shadow. She then ran some tinted lip gloss across her average lips and viewed herself in the mirror. She wondered, *How many months had passed by since she prepared to go somewhere? Was the last time she'd dressed for anything the day they were planning to go out to eat together? No,* she reminded herself, *it was the funeral.* She thought about that day for a few seconds and realized just how much time was lost. Suzanne was never very confident when she dressed, she was never sure if she looked okay. Paul always validated her appearance and her choice of clothing and he would tell her if he liked something or not. She relied on him more than she realized. But she was on her own now. As she finished up and began putting things away, she wondered to herself why she did not offer to just make the coffee, but realized she simply wasn't thinking clearly.

After agreeing to eat lunch together, the two women gathered their coats and purses and climbed in to Catherine's no-nonsense, grey Volvo and ventured down the street to the nearby lunch spot that Catherine was familiar with. It was quiet and early enough that they were able to land a booth. The server was friendly and accommodated their need for private conversation. She took their order and brought out their ice teas. They proceeded to order and soon their salads arrived. They stayed in the booth talking until the busy waitress' frequent visits asking if she could get them anything else let them know they needed to give up their table. Catherine insisted on paying the bill and left a hefty tip for the patient server and they headed back to the car. Back in the safety of the car, Suzanne finally gave herself permission to cry and when she did, Catherine reached over and touched her on the shoulder. It was cold outside and Catherine would turn the car on periodically to warm them. Catherine was very attentive and kind and she eventually asked Suzanne if she would mind if she prayed for her; Suzanne agreed. When Catherine prayed for Suzanne, she felt it was finally the beginning of something positive and Suzanne felt a glimmer of hope that day.

While sitting in the parking lot, it became time to pick up the girls. Suzanne couldn't believe how long they'd talked. She also could not believe this woman, almost a complete stranger, gave her one whole day of her time. But Suzanne was so relieved and ready to unload and let her feelings out. *It felt like it was the beginning of her prayer being answered*.

Catherine simply listened to Suzanne talk. She never said much, certainly not pretending to know what Suzanne was going through because she knew she had never been through anything like the death of a husband. She relied on her faith though and when she could, trying not to sound too cliché or give pat answers, she would insert encouraging words to assure Suzanne that God did love her and that He would help her through this. She didn't want to preach, but she knew God was the only answer for Suzanne. Her faith in God was strong, but Catherine wondered how strong her faith would be if her husband were suddenly killed? She felt that Suzanne was still angry, but she also sensed her faith was still present. She just needed to help her rekindle it somehow.

Much to Erin's surprise, her mother was sitting in

the passenger side of the car when Christy's mom picked them up that day. Two weeks had passed since the *abortion*. Suddenly, she panicked and thought that somehow her mother found out. Erin looked directly at her mother and said, "What are you doing here?" Suzanne met Erin's eyes and held her gaze for a few seconds, and said very quietly, "I'm trying to live." Erin quickly looked away and mumbled "whatever" under her breath. Then they all rode home lost in their thoughts.

Catherine tried to make conversation. She was always asking Christy questions about her day or homework or church. It was odd to both the girls for Erin's mom to be in the car dressed with makeup on sitting in the passenger seat. That put Christy and Erin in the backseat sitting side-by-side and even that was a little weird. The presence of Erin's mom changed their predictable routine.

Catherine pulled into Suzanne and Erin's driveway and dropped them off. As Suzanne exited the car, she thanked Catherine for her time that day and when she grasped the car handle to close the door, Catherine asked if Suzanne would like to have coffee another day. Suzanne laughed and said, "Just coffee?" They agreed to meet again the following week. When Suzanne walked back in the house that day, she felt lighter and somewhat hopeful. She realized that was the first time she'd laughed in a very long time. When she turned to look for Erin, she'd already disappeared into the house, leaving the front door wide open.

Suzanne and Catherine continued meeting for

coffee and lunches. All the while, Catherine simply listened, supported and encouraged her. Suzanne finally scheduled a session with a grief counselor upon Catherine's suggestion. She met with some of the staff at the church they both attended as well. She began going back to church and met some of the other women at a Tuesday morning Bible study. It was hard, she felt so out of place, now that she was single. Soon though, she was functioning again. She knew her life would never be the same but she began to have a routine. She began making healthy meals again, cleaning the house and driving Erin to school and back. Sometimes Christy rode with them and she and Catherine began to trade off taking and picking up the girls.

Her daughter had really changed these past few months. Suzanne felt like a failure as a mom. She could barely remember the last few months, and when she did remember, she was embarrassed. She was aware that Erin dated a boy back in the fall whom she'd met at school this year. She did not even know his name, but she figured they broke up back in January around the time she and Catherine started going for coffee. She had lost so many weeks and months. Erin seemed a lot more distant now but who was she kidding? She was an absentee mother. When she tried to make a rule, or tell her anything now, Erin would just roll her eyes and say, "Are you kidding me?" She didn't listen anymore; she did what she wanted. She was about as distant as the stars.

Suzanne realized that relationships were strange and unpredictable so she began to work on her relationship with the Lord; she wanted closeness and intimacy with Him. She knew ultimately, she could only rely on Him. When Suzanne began to peel back the layers of hurt and fear and allow God to begin to heal her broken heart, she began the painful process of going through Paul's things. Upon doing so, she discovered things that disturbed her and caused her to wonder what kind of man she was married to … she wondered if Paul was really ever a Christian, a true believer? He was a good father and a good husband and a wonderful provider but the things she saw when she rifled through his belongings caused her to wonder about whether he ever experienced a true relationship with Christ. And then she reflected on all those times she tried to talk to him about Jesus … he would always become agitated for her pressing in on him. He went to church, but that was it. She remembered how she wished they could have prayed together as a family. And she went back to the day she shared her salvation experience with him; he did not say anything other than, "Sure, I believe in God." Yet, she knew that was not enough, Jesus was the only way to the Father. How did she miss all these signals when he was alive?

And Erin? She just didn't know, but she knew she was not the judge. And thank God, she wasn't! But Suzanne wanted to start fresh. Erin was almost sixteen and she only had a couple more years of high school left. Suzanne was beginning to move past the pain of losing Paul. Now, she wanted to help Erin move forward too. She wanted to get her to see a counselor soon. But it never happened. Erin would not go.

She started driver's training in the spring, turned sixteen in September and began driving herself to school as soon as she was able obtain her license. Suzanne began working and Erin began working too. Suzanne used some of the insurance money from the accident to help buy a car for Erin hoping that would help with their strained relationship, but it didn't. The gulf between them grew wider. She was aware that Erin dated some but she was private and didn't share. Of course, Erin obeyed her mother's rules and cooperated by coming in by the designated curfew. Even though they lived in the same household, they weren't close. Something was lost and Suzanne could not get it back. When she would try to talk to Erin or ask her to eat dinner with her, Erin would just tell her she was busy with school or work or friends and Suzanne did not have a choice other than to accept it because of the guilt she felt. On good days, they began to discuss college. She was glad Erin wanted to further her education. Suzanne was worried about Erin's grades though. She began checking into state schools and realized due to Erin's grades there was no way she would be accepted. Erin's only hope would be to start at a technical school and possibly transfer to a state school after a year or two.

The thing that bugged Suzanne the most about her relationship with Erin was not that she didn't want to hang out with her; she knew this was normal. She'd talked to Catherine and other moms and everyone said the same thing, "They're trying to find out who they are. They don't want their parents around." No, what bothered Suzanne was how Erin dressed and the boys she chose to be around. Erin and Christy were still friends, and she was glad about that, but every time she would see her come out of her room with a new outfit on or get a glimpse of a boy Erin was talking with or dated, she would always think to herself, "Really?" Never in a million years did she expect Erin would choose such clothing or the guys who looked and dressed like they did. And if she tried to talk to Erin about how she dressed or boys—forget it. Usually, Erin would just roll her eyes and say, "Mom, you don't know what you're talking about." So, Suzanne would leave it alone. She hoped she could just get her through high school and then college. She didn't think Erin was too interested in any one particular guy. She didn't seem to have much of a passion for anything. She did not think she was happy either and that bothered her. But she wasn't really happy either; she was still trying to figure all of this out. She wished so badly she could rewind the clock and go back to when Paul died and handle things differently. But she could not. Those days were gone.

After Suzanne recovered emotionally and spiritually, she realized that condemnation and guilt were the thought processes that held her back and would continue to if she let herself dwell on them. She now knew God had always been there and was there for her now. Yet, the worst part of her depression she thought, when she looked back, was the isolation and false beliefs that she created in her own mind. After Paul's death, she began to believe that God wasn't there for her and never had been. She falsely believed Paul was there for her, but not God. And then, she somehow convinced herself that Paul was gone because God was punishing her for something she deserved and He didn't care anything at all about her or her future. It was the loneliest place in the world to be and each lie was perpetuated by another.

Once she turned her thinking around, which was in itself a big spiritual process, she was able to reshape her life and begin to understand the truth of who God really is. Her thoughts were a huge part of it. She memorized Romans 12:2 which says, *"Let God transform you into a new person by changing the way you think."* She began to realize that God did care for her and her future.

Another part of her healing was reading her Bible and allowing God's word to feed her broken spirit. She even started going to Al-anon meetings at the suggestion of the counselor she talked with. She never knew how much her father's alcoholism shaped and influenced her life and her behavior until now. The meetings helped her to pursue her own happiness and to realize she was not responsible for everyone and everything.

She learned a lot in those meetings and when she felt like she was trying to control things too much, she would practice the steps. She prayed the Serenity Prayer often. "God, grant me the serenity to accept the things I cannot change, the courage to change the things I can; and the wisdom to know the difference." It was simply a prayer of letting go and realizing "God is God!" She is just a human being made of flesh and blood and all she could do was accept herself and others ... but not control. She thought about Erin and how she wanted to change so many things about her—but she could not. God could, but she could not.

The only thing she could change was herself. She could change her behavior and so she tried every day not to be codependent by helping, fixing and rescuing others. In the past, she always thought she could fix other people when really, she was the one who needed fixing and changing. She was learning that all those other people needed to fix themselves with God's help. It sounded a little cold at first, but she realized that when you try to help, fix and rescue others, you are simply skirting around the fact that your own issues don't exist. You end up putting yourself and all the things that need fixing about yourself on the last rung of the ladder. Suzanne realized that when she did that, she was not facing what she needed to face. It reminded her of the Scripture in the Bible which says, "Why do you look at the speck of sawdust in your brother's eye and pay no attention to the plank in your own eye?" (Matthew 7:3) She had certainly done that long enough and was now ready to work on the many boards in her own life and leave the specks for those with them. She realized everyone was on their own journey and their own path.

Each day, she did her very best to spend time alone praying, reading and journaling. She made an effort to read Scripture even if it was just one Psalm or Proverb. It fed her spiritual hunger for God. She would chew on the verses and ponder what they said. She applied them to her life as best she could and throughout the day, she simply talked to God about everything.

Mistakes and Sins

If we claim we have no sin,
we are only fooling ourselves
and not living in the truth.
1 John 1:8

Suzanne
April, 1994

"Mom," said Erin anxiously, "I *need* to talk to you."

Suzanne was just arriving home from her job at the Christian school that was connected to the church she and Erin attended together. She finally felt emotionally stable after the counseling she received, along with the fact that three years had passed since Paul's untimely death. Suzanne accepted this new phase of her life and had put it back together as best she could. She discovered a new normal that consisted of being employed as a teacher which helped financially. She had a healthy routine now and she was working on finding her happiness again.

But Suzanne was tired. She was now approaching forty-three and Erin was seventeen. She couldn't believe it. The last three years truly took a toll on her. It was difficult to be the sole provider for their family, especially with Erin beginning college in the fall. From time to time she would reminisce about her life with Paul prior to his death. How well he took care of them. It was a long time before she became financially stable again.

After about a year passed, and she processed through her grief, Suzanne began to pursue employment. Thankfully, Paul did have some life insurance, though it was not enough. She often wondered why Paul didn't take out a larger policy. When Erin was little, Suzanne did not work much out of the home except for volunteering in the community and sometimes at her church for special events. She did a little bit of substitute teaching. After Paul died, they lived over a year on the insurance money, but it began to dwindle, making her fearful. She paid for all the funeral expenses and hospital bills with a portion of it. Then, with what was left over, she continued to pay the monthly mortgage and other bills so they could remain in their home and then later she bought a car for Erin. Suzanne purchased Erin's car hoping to compensate for the guilt she felt for all those months she was a non-existent mother. She knew it was extravagant to buy a car for Erin with her shrinking finances even though she chose a Honda Civic with no extra equipment. Suzanne was sensible enough to know that she needed to move. However, with the real estate market still in recovery mode, she wasn't sure how she would come out. The three of them had enjoyed their new home for only about six months before Paul died. So, she opted to pay the larger mortgage and struggle through. The money was disappearing quickly though, and she wanted to have some left to help put Erin through college. Thankfully, the church she attended was large and there was a Christian School K-8th grade connected to it. They helped her out a couple of years ago, first by allowing her to substitute teach while she worked on her recertification and then, when a teaching spot became available, they'd hired her as part of their staff.

As Suzanne's friendship with Catherine grew, she urged her to go to counseling and seek some desperately needed help. They also connected her up to a weekly grief class and it helped. She also began attending regular worship services and became a member and made some new friends. Erin came to church some, but not as often as Suzanne wished. Erin was working too, mostly after school and on weekends at the mall. She drove herself to and from school and work and Suzanne was thankful she could buy a dependable car for her. She was thankful for all God was doing in her life but she was still very tired and overwhelmed. It was still not easy. She could not help but look back at how things were when Paul was alive. Her counselor shared the Scripture with her about forgetting the past and looking forward to what lies ahead[12], but every now and then, Suzanne just could not help looking back and wondering what *could have been.*

Church was a positive experience for Suzanne once she finally started attending again. Going regularly really helped her get back on her feet emotionally and spiritually. She was grateful to the body of Christ. She thought about the analogy used for the body of Christ and how all believers working together make up Christ's body,[13] whether seen or unseen, each had a job to do. If anything at all happened that was positive since Paul's death, Suzanne could honestly say she was growing spiritually. Before Paul died, she was saved but she wasn't very committed to the Lord or to church.

So, when the teaching job became available and was offered to her, she felt it was an answer to prayer. At first, she felt underqualified, but she was catching on quickly, becoming more confident with time. She was pretty comfortable around the other teachers. Her personal life merged with her job now, but that was okay. These people were more than co-workers, they were her friends, some even attended church with her. But Suzanne did not know how much pride she possessed until her daughter Erin sought her out that spring day.

Erin was scheduled to graduate in May and Suzanne began budgeting for her to go to Atlanta Tech, Erin's only choice with her grades. She was planning on a business major like her father. She was already offered a job from her father's former business partner, Jim, who had worked with Paul and knew their family. He generously proposed to help Erin get started in her career by providing her with her first professional position. He owned a string of small commercial buildings and offered to hire her as one of his managers. Erin simply must earn her degree. She was excited and held an optimistic vision for her future. She barely made it through the last three years of high school because of her delicate emotional state. Once Suzanne dealt with her own grief, she tried to focus on Erin and get help for her too, but she rejected it. She told her mom she didn't need it. She was the one who took care of herself and said condescending things like, "Did you not notice I was the one who held it together, doing everything from the cooking to the laundry while you sat on the sofa like a zombie?"

Suzanne did remember and she was guilt-ridden over those months that were lost. She had not parented her daughter. *She abandoned her*. And a lot of damage was done. She didn't know how much. She prayed for her every day and wondered, *Was it too late?* She and Catherine talked some about Erin, but it was a touchy subject. She didn't want to hear the things Catherine told her. For instance, all those nights she thought Erin was with Christy at Catherine's house, she really wasn't. *Where had she been?*, Suzanne wondered but she couldn't ask now. She missed her window of opportunity. And these last couple of years, Erin dated a lot of boys. There was a void in her life and it was obvious to Suzanne that her daughter craved male attention. She watched how she responded to boys and felt her daughter was a little more seductive than was appropriate in how she dressed and acted. She thought about Paul and wondered what he would have said about some of her outfits, hairstyles and makeup. *How would Paul have handled this?*

Erin's grades were not satisfactory either. If

compared to before Paul's death to after Paul's death, it was like night and day. When Erin graduated, even a state school would be out of the question. So, a local tech school was as good as it would get for her for now. But she could still start fresh. Suzanne was hopeful. When Erin finished high school, she would be on her way to college. She would earn a BA in Business. It wouldn't take long. They could focus on it together.

Suzanne felt Erin had healed from her father's death as well as anyone could heal from something so tragic. They could both begin to see the light at the end of the tunnel. Suzanne was excited for Erin, not so much for herself because she still missed Paul and being married and all that went with it, but at least her daughter could have a promising future ahead of her. She would think about selling the house when Erin finished school and hopefully she could get on her feet financially one day soon. She even thought about dating, but that was still a long way off. Paul had been gone for three years now. Suzanne was learning to live as a single mom, a single woman, and being the sole provider for the two of them which was not easy.

Paul's death was hard on Erin in a different way. She was such a "daddy's girl." He always made her feel special and he adored his daughter. Suzanne loved the fact they possessed such an exceptional relationship. It seemed that all through Erin's early years, Paul helped guide Erin and they experienced very few blowups. Even when Erin was on the cusp of becoming a teenager, there seemed to be very little rebellion compared to other kids, based on what her circle of mom-friends confided to her back then. Paul would take Erin out almost every Sunday afternoons for a father/daughter date.

Sometimes Erin and Paul would go to a movie and they would always eat junk food, arriving home stuffed with no appetite for dinner. Other times, they might go to the mall and Paul would purchase a new outfit for Erin, usually spending a whole lot more than what Suzanne was willing to spend. The main thing was they had this awesome father/daughter relationship and Paul listened to and respected his daughter. Erin loved and respected her father and anytime she needed advice, she waited to ask him. She and her mother were close back then too, but their relationship was different. Suzanne was delighted that Paul and Erin were so close. She never experienced that with her own father and couldn't even begin to imagine what it would be like to have a father who desired to spend time with her. Her own father's alcoholism determined their relationship; and well—*how do you get close to an alcoholic father?* She suffered a lot in her childhood and knew that she still carried a lot of emotional baggage, but she was doing as best she could.

Erin recently started dating a guy named Joe, who Suzanne loathed. She did not think Paul would have approved of him. She sure didn't. He was older than Erin and that bugged her too. Her idea of who Erin would end up with sure wasn't him. There were visible tattoos and piercings which she loathed. She knew she was old school, but aside from the way Joe *looked*, it was how he *treated* Erin. He didn't treat her as if she were special and felt Erin was settling for so much less than what she deserved. She figured this wouldn't last and Erin would graduate high school and move on. By the time she started college in the fall, she hoped Erin would be over him. She hoped Erin would meet someone who would love her the way Paul loved her. She wanted everything parents want for their daughters. She secretly kept her eye on a boy from their church whom she thought would be perfect for Erin. His name was Michael, and he didn't come often because he was in college. But Suzanne thought he seemed like the type of guy she could picture Erin with. Not that church attendance would guarantee anything, but at least it was a start, better than this "Joe" guy. Joe was not even close to what she expected or hoped for Erin.

Suzanne's thoughts were abruptly interrupted when Erin said softly, "Mom, I'm pregnant." Suzanne thought she heard Erin say that she was pregnant, and at the same time she felt the blood rush to her head combined with a feeling of lightheadedness. She began to tremble. She could not process this information as her thoughts came rushing in and the dreaded feeling of things being out of control, way out of her control. All that counseling, all those meetings, all the Scripture she memorized could not prepare her for this.

Then she heard herself saying very loudly and in a very strange voice, *"Pregnant? What do you mean, pregnant?"* Erin hung back and started to respond to her mother's outburst, but Suzanne interrupted her. The voice she heard was not the voice she recognized as her own, "You can't be pregnant!" Erin answered her by pulling out a pregnancy stick and waving it in front of her. "Mom," Erin answered, "These things don't lie; it's not a mistake. I mean yeah, I made a mistake and now this thing says I'm pregnant." Suzanne replied, "How ... who ... what? Are you serious?" Erin quickly began talking, "Mom, listen to me, I can have the baby, and everything will be okay." Her words trailed off as though she were trying to convince her of something as simple as giving her some money for a new outfit, "If you help me, you know?"

Suzanne suddenly felt as helpless as she did the night Paul died. Everything she planned for her life and for Erin's was being taken away again, stripped from her. Suzanne's life was again being jerked out from under her like a rug without her consent. She was back on her feet and they were finally making it. *They were making it.* Yet, now she felt like she was being thrown down to the ground again just like that fateful night Paul died. She couldn't think, she could not believe this. Suzanne gasped and thought to herself, *No! She would not let her life be ruined again and surely not her daughter's. She knew Joe was a jerk.* Suddenly, she grabbed Erin by her shoulders and snapped at her, "No, this is not okay, what do you mean, it will be okay? How could you do this to me Erin? You can't embarrass us like this. You can't have a baby! What are you thinking? Why on earth would you do this to yourself?" As the words tumbled out of her mouth, they seemed foreign to her. It was like they were coming from someone else. She was a Christian and always tried to be self-controlled. She could see the shock on Erin's face as well as she stood motionless. But this was blowing Suzanne away, she was horrified, appalled and shocked, *This is crazy,* she thought. Never in her wildest imagination did she think this could happen to her daughter, not now, not after everything that had already happened. Not after everything they had both been through. Paul's death was an accident, completely out of her control. She finally made her peace with God and stopped blaming Him for it. She went through counseling and finally felt their lives were stable again. Erin was okay, too, at least she thought she was. And now, here Erin stood in front of her informing her in the most nonchalant and carefree way that *she was pregnant!* Her daughter, who she'd been through so much with, was now pregnant and just seventeen. She was almost ready to graduate! And here she was, on staff at a Christian school with a pregnant, unmarried daughter. Seriously? She could not believe it.

And so, Suzanne began to lose it. She knew she was screaming and yelling and out of control; yet, she just kept at it. She heard herself shouting and saying things she knew Christian women shouldn't say.

"I won't support you Erin, I will not stand behind this!" And, in the middle of her shouting, she was asking herself way back in the recesses of her mind, *How could I even have these thoughts, much less say them?*

"I won't help you. I won't pay for your school. I will

not support you or this child. Then what will you do? Joe can't support you." Then she saw the look on Erin's face, she saw the disappointment in her tear-filled eyes as she turned away from her. When she looked at Erin again, she saw she was crying. Then, she heard Erin speak.

"Mom," Erin said in a hushed tone, "Joe's gone, I told him a couple of weeks ago and he left. He doesn't want a baby or the responsibility. I haven't heard from him since the day I told him. But Mom," Erin begged, "I really want to have this baby. Please don't say you won't help me." When Suzanne heard Erin's plea, she panicked even more. *Joe was gone? Her daughter was pregnant, the guy is gone, and she is still in high school?* She began to feel lightheaded, as if she were underwater. She heard herself from way down beneath as she yelled even louder, "Erin, I cannot afford to take care of a newborn baby and you. What will people think? I work on staff at a Christian school for heaven's sake. Are you kidding me? Would you really be that selfish to ruin my reputation in our church and in this community? After everything we've been through? These people have helped us so much. Think about it Erin, what would your dad think?"

She saw Erin's face, and inside Suzanne was dying. She saw how bad she was hurting Erin but she didn't care. She would not allow this to happen. She couldn't help what happened the night Paul died but she could certainly do something about this.

Then she calmed herself down. She gathered her thoughts and very firmly and very quietly she heard herself say to Erin, "You should have an abortion or you will be out on your own. I am done. I didn't sign up for this." As she heard herself, in the back of her mind, she couldn't believe what she heard coming out of her own mouth. But she felt she did not have another choice. There was no choice. Erin had not given her a choice. Yes, in her clouded thinking, abortion was the only choice.

She turned and walked out of the room into the den where she nervously sat down on the sofa and stared in a daze at the TV for the rest of the evening. Sometime later that night, while she was staring mindlessly at the TV, she heard Erin leave the house, quietly closing the door behind her. At that moment, she did not even care where she was going. She was back in her familiar spot on the sofa staring into nothingness, her dreams for herself and Erin were being ripped apart once again and shredded to pieces.

She finally got up around 2:30 a.m. and went to bed. She slept very little, her thoughts consumed her. She kept thinking, *How could this happen?* and *Why us?* and *Why does Erin want a baby?* She wondered about Erin's career and the money she set aside to help her start college. She knew it wasn't much but it was Erin's dream, right? She scraped and budgeted just to have the money to put her through school. She thought, *Doesn't she care about her future? Doesn't she care about me? Doesn't she want a normal life? Why would she go and get pregnant?* Her final thought before drifting off to sleep was, *Where is God in all of this ... and why, God, why?*

Déjà Vu

*For we all fall short
of God's glorious standard.*

Romans 3:23

Erin and Suzanne

April, 1994

Erin thought a lot about this baby. She also thought a lot about her other baby. She did not want to go through this again. Yet she couldn't tell her mom about before. She just couldn't. She wanted this baby. She really did. How could she go and do that again? But she did.

It was a rainy April morning when she and her mother drove up to the exact same clinic she went to before. This time her real name was given. Her mother made the appointment. There were girls in there just like before. She saw a guy and a girl and wondered about this couple, *If they love each other, why are they doing this?*

She could understand all these young, single girls in here without anyone at all; she remembered her feeling of helplessness when she'd come before, but why would two people who love each other choose to be here?

Erin was giving her mom only yes and no answers. She did not have anything to say to her. Suzanne asked her if she'd eaten, if she'd called work and if her homework was done. Erin couldn't believe it. *Did she do her homework?* She did not know how she was going to get through this. She already grieved so much for the baby she aborted two years ago. She swore she would never get pregnant again until she was married—swore she would never have another abortion. But here she was. She was driven by her *mommy* to the abortion clinic. Her own mother, who was supposed to be such a *good Christian,* someone who worked at a Christian school was bringing her to an abortion clinic. Erin thought, *She's only worried about her reputation, but not me. She couldn't care less about me and what I'm going through. And this is her grandchild she wants me to abort.* Erin could go have the child, but Joe didn't want the baby either. Erin was the only one who wanted this baby but the cold stone fact was she could not support herself. She needed her mom so she could go to college. *Why was her mother treating her like this?* She couldn't believe it. She would never forgive her for this.

When Suzanne rose that morning, the day Erin was scheduled to have the abortion, she made herself a cup of coffee and sat down to quietly read her devotional for that day. But she felt stupid doing that, so she tossed the little book off to the side in her anger.

She called in to work the night before and told them she wasn't feeling well and would not be in the following day. She called Erin's school that morning to inform them of a doctor's appointment. She woke Erin soon after she showered and dressed and they set out together to find the clinic Suzanne located in the phone book. She did not recognize the address and was a little nervous as they entered the part of town where it was located. She had no idea a medical office would be in this area of town. Was she naive or just misinformed? But the streets didn't get any better as they travelled along and the buildings became more and more dilapidated. She squirmed a bit in her seat and soon they arrived at the clinic. It was a small building that didn't seem to her like a professional medical building or a doctor's office. It was stuck in the middle of the worst area of town and there was nothing nice about it. There was a stressed-out receptionist taking names while handing out pregnancy tests and pointing them in the direction of the bathroom so they could confirm their condition before paying their fee. There were several young women in the waiting area, and Suzanne noticed that most of them were alone. One sat with a boyfriend or maybe it was her husband. There weren't very many older women. They all looked like young girls, just like Erin. Most of them seemed reserved or withdrawn.

Suzanne handed Erin an envelope with the correct amount of cash after she finished taking the test that obviously confirmed her pregnancy and sent her to check in. Suzanne then turned to look for somewhere to sit down and found two empty chairs side by side; she tossed her purse in the empty chair and grabbed a magazine and sat in the remaining one. Erin went to the window and checked in with the receptionist sitting behind the glass. She gave the woman her name, this time her real name, handed her the envelope with the money inside. When she finished at the window, she came back and sat down a few chairs away from her mom. Suzanne glanced up. When she saw that Erin chose to sit away from her, she ached inside. When she saw the look in Erin's eyes, she quickly averted her eyes back to the magazine. She kept thinking, *This is no big deal, having a baby will ruin her life. It is legal.* She remembered back to when the Supreme Court passed Roe v. Wade. She thought and thought about it. Somewhere way back in her mind she remembered hearing a preacher say something about man's laws versus God's laws and a doorway of doubt was slightly opened. Surely God would understand.

It seemed like hours. Names were called. Erin could not concentrate. She kept thinking, my baby is inside me and is growing and forming. I am protecting it and in just a few minutes I am going to let someone suck it out of me and throw it in the garbage. She teared up a few times. And then her name was called.

When Suzanne heard Erin's name called, she looked up and quickly stood. She then walked over to where Erin was still sitting and very quietly, said, "Erin, this will all be over soon and everything will be fine. This is best." Erin just gave her mom a look and stood up taking nothing with her and walked away. She walked over to the door where the woman stood with her manila file folder, her back against the open door; the woman greeted Erin with a sunny smile and everything was—just like before.

When it was over and Erin was cleared to leave, they called her mother in from the waiting room to escort Erin out the back door. A prescription was given to her this time for her pain, but it would not help with the real pain. Her mother tried to help Erin, but she refused to let her. They both walked to the car in silence and her mother drove her home. Erin cried all the way home with her face turned toward the passenger window. She felt so empty—and she was. She was emptied out of the life that was inside her and she felt a void that she did not think would ever go away. Would she ever get over this? Would she ever be able to forgive her mother? Would she ever have a child? Her mother said, "When we get home, just rest. You can stay home tomorrow, and you'll be okay by Monday." How did her mother think she would be okay? She realized her mother was very okay, now that she could go back to her hypocritical life, working at the Christian school with all those perfect Christian people.

When she arrived home, her mother tried to assist her but Erin refused. Erin very matter-of-factly stated, "I'm fine Mother, just leave me alone. You said I would be fine, so I'm fine. I am going to lie down." Her stomach cramped and she was bleeding. She went to her room and threw herself across her bed. She cried until she went to sleep. When she woke, it was dark. She got up and went to the kitchen. Her mother had already gone to bed and left some food that could be reheated in the microwave with a note that said, "Erin, I am sorry you are upset with me. Please try and understand I only want what's best for you. I truly love you, Mom." She tossed the note and the food in the trash. She retrieved a glass from the cabinet, filled it with water, and went back to bed.

Suzanne woke up early. She made a cup of coffee and went to open her Bible. *Hypocrite* was all she heard. She closed the Book. She went to Erin's room and looked in on her. She was sleeping peacefully. When she went back through the kitchen, she saw the trash can with the food in it and the note on top. *Hypocrite,* she heard again. *You are not a Christian. Christians don't behave this way. You are a murderer! You murdered your own grandchild! It's all your fault. Things will never be the same for you or Erin.* She continued to hear the condemning voice, *You wanted to fix your relationship with her. Well you certainly have fixed it. You will never have a relationship with your daughter. YOU ARE A MURDERER!*

She went to take a shower. She tried to think of something else but she couldn't. All she could think of was what a huge mistake she'd made.

She reminded herself this was legal, the Supreme Court made it so. And then she remembered that quote, "Man's laws cannot make moral what God has declared immoral." Hmmm … and the doorway of doubt opened wider. She left the house and drove to work in a fog.

When Suzanne arrived at work, she felt even more alone. There was no one there that she felt she could talk with, not about this. If she confessed Erin's pregnancy, no one would understand. If she confessed that she encouraged Erin to have an abortion, they wouldn't understand. So, she just closed everyone off. If anyone said anything to her or commented on her quiet behavior, she would simply claim she was tired and that wasn't a lie. She was so very tired. She laid awake all night thinking of what she did. It was too late to change her mind; it was over and she could not change her decision or go backwards or think about a different solution.

Would Erin ever forgive her? The problem was gone, but what about how she felt now? She felt no better. And what about Erin? She thought that *afterwards* they would both feel relieved, but she sure didn't. She thought they could both go back to their normal lives. Would Erin ever be able to get over this? What kind of emotional damage was done to her? She didn't know. She just didn't know.

When she walked in the teacher's lounge, everyone present asked how she was feeling. She almost forgot she called in sick the day before. *Liar,* she heard in her mind. *You are a liar! What are you doing working in a church?* She heard these voices condemning her and accusing her. "Oh, fine," she said, "a twenty-four-hour thing," she answered, "I'm good now." She told all who asked that day that she was fine, but she was quiet all day. Most of her coworkers thought she was still feeling weak and tired from the virus she'd said she got, so not too much was said. She went through the motions of the day and could not wait to leave.

When she arrived home, Erin had already left. She was surprised that she was out of bed and gone. For the next few days, Erin avoided her and Suzanne was actually very okay with that. Every time she thought of Erin and what she had basically forced her to do. She heard condemning, accusing voices and she wholeheartedly agreed with the voices. Suzanne stopped praying and reading her Bible.

She did not feel worthy to talk to God about this. She was a hypocrite. There is no way she could have done this and still be a Christian. She could not. God could not love her. She was miserable and alone. So, she would do her best to put it out of her mind. A few days went by. Erin was fine. She went to bed that first day and then she seemed okay after that. Quiet, yes. But surely, she would be fine. She would go back to school on Monday and get on with things. Graduation was very soon, and she would get caught up in the end-of-year activities.

Suzanne hated Joe. And Suzanne felt God hated her ... so she simply stopped praying altogether.

Amazing Grace

Have mercy on me, O God,
because of your unfailing love.

Because of your great compassion,
blot out the stain of my sins.

Wash me clean from my guilt.

Purify me from my sin.

For I recognize my rebellion;
it haunts me day and night.

Against you, and you alone,
have I sinned.

Psalms 51:1-4

Suzanne and Catherine

May, 1994

Suzanne and Catherine's friendship grew when Catherine helped Suzanne walk through her depression in those first months after Paul died. Catherine showed up at just the right time; really, she just kept showing up until Suzanne finally allowed the pain and suffering she locked behind the very high wall that she alone constructed to be exposed. Talking things out with another woman who was also a believer created a close bond between them and their daughters were good friends as well.

Suzanne was still somewhat intimidated by Catherine; her faith was solid. Sometimes, she would create a bit of a distance between them when she felt insecure that way. It wasn't Catherine though; it was Suzanne's lack of confidence—and it began way back when she was little.

After Erin's abortion, Suzanne was so worried that someone would find out. She concocted and invented as many reasons as she possibly could to create a safe distance between she and Catherine. She claimed to be busy because of Erin's upcoming graduation, and she thought up as many reasons as she could to not spend time with her friend. She kept phone conversations very brief which helped her keep the distance between them. Because she worked full time and Catherine did not, it was not that difficult.

She knew Catherine was busy with Christy's graduation too. She heard her mention several times about their summer plans, and she was sure that Catherine was also helping Christy prepare for college in the fall. Christy, being a very good student, was accepted to a state school and, hopefully after Erin attended a tech school for a year or two, she, too, would follow.

Suzanne felt she was walking on eggshells these days. Life was so uncertain. She felt that she could not rely on anyone or anything. She was angry with God, angry with herself, and she was even angry with Erin.

Plus, she hated Joe. Moreover, Suzanne was certain that God was mad at her for what she had done.

Her thoughts were rooted in guilt. The days seemed to continue endlessly because she walked around carrying a burden of shame and guilt. The burden was oppressive, hovering over her, engulfing her, and ever-accusing her of her sin.

However, one day when she could not listen to the thoughts inside of her head any longer, nor deal with the shame and the guilt another minute, she decided she must talk to someone. Who better than Catherine? The thing about Catherine was, she never treated Suzanne like she was superior to her and did not have a holier-than-thou attitude. How Suzanne felt about Catherine was really her problem ... she knew she was the one with the issues. Catherine never gave Suzanne any reason to feel judged by her. She was always encouraging. Suzanne felt that Catherine's faith was strong, and she always seemed to have everything together. Suzanne didn't even feel like a Christian anymore. Christians simply did not do things like she had done.

But she was her friend and she needed a friend right now. So, Suzanne called her up and asked if they could meet for lunch. Catherine was always accommodating and never made Suzanne feel as though she were burdensome.

So, they agreed to meet on Saturday morning at the little restaurant they both knew about, which was halfway between them. It was the same restaurant they went to the day she'd poured her heart out to

Catherine about Paul when she felt so abandoned by God.

Now, here she was again, but this time, she felt *she* was the devil. She felt she was the epitome of evil. She could not feel anything but condemning thoughts about herself. She was heartsick about what she'd done ... what she'd practically forced Erin to do. She put pressure on Erin to kill her child. Erin's baby, her grandchild. She was an accessory to murderer. She helped to kill her first grandchild.

But what happened that day was miraculous for Suzanne. She told Catherine everything. She confessed her sin to her friend[14] and told her about Erin's desire to have the baby. She'd told her how she drove Erin, forced her really, to go to an abortion clinic; and while she sat in a crappy plastic chair in a dumpy waiting area reading a magazine, she paid for her first grandchild to be destroyed, murdered by a doctor and thrown away in a garbage can.

Instead of seeing shock or surprise upon Catherine's face, thinking she'd just dropped a bombshell of information on her friend that she would be unable to process, Catherine simply said, "Suzanne, everyone makes mistakes. We all sin," and then she said, "It's so obvious to me that you're sorry. You feel genuine remorse. God certainly knows your heart." She met her eyes and looked deep into them as she held her gaze, "It seems as though you have been convicted since the very day it happened, and there is absolutely nothing you can do about it now. You can't undo it," and then she added very softly,

"But, you can do this. You can take this to God, repent and ask for His forgiveness." Catherine then told her what she'd needed to hear, "Suzanne, if you confess your sin and ask God to forgive you, He will forgive you."[15] Then she added, "Receive His forgiveness and be free from the guilt; that's why Jesus died—*to set us free*."[16]

Then Catherine told Suzanne a story that blew Suzanne's mind. Catherine confided to Suzanne that she too had an abortion before she married her soon-to-be husband, Bill. She told her of how he pressured her to have sex. She was so ashamed of becoming pregnant that she wanted to have the abortion as much as he did. She thought the shame of everyone knowing she was pregnant would be worse than secretly having an abortion. They both attended church together, and their families knew each other. She was only twenty. So, she and Bill went together to a clinic thinking it would solve all their problems, but instead, they both struggled from the outset with unbearable shame and guilt. They almost broke up. They cried and cried together and alone. They questioned their faith and talked honestly about it. They asked each other with no accusation, how does a Christian make a decision like this? They condemned themselves over and over until finally, when they could not deal with the pain anymore, they talked with Bill's parents who surprisingly did not condemn them, but instead laid out the Scriptures for them about sin and forgiveness.

Catherine was convicted and finally confessed her sin to God to received His forgiveness. Bill too owned up to his part in all of it and sought God's forgiveness. They both came through it together but their repentance was just between God and them. He cleaned their souls and strengthened their faith in Him. When they were finally able to deal with it, they forgave one another for the part each one played in the creation and destruction of their first child.

At the advice of Bill's mother, they sought counseling together as well as separately. It helped them prior to their marriage. After marrying, they considered their daughter, Christy, a gift from God. And they were both so very thankful for her. They never talked with Catherine's parents about it though. Catherine just could not do it and asked Bill's mom, now her mother-in-law, to never tell. True to her promise she never said anything. She then added that sin is inevitable as long as we are alive; being a Christian does not exempt us from sin. It's what we do with it that sets us apart as Christians.

Before this meeting with Catherine, deep down in her soul, Suzanne thought what she would hear from her friend was a person confirming to her how truly evil she was. She found herself even wanting someone to agree with all the voices she continued hearing in her head these last few weeks about what a terrible mother she was; how she should never ever call herself a Christian; and how she was a murderer; *how she ruined Erin's life; and how she was most likely going to hell.*

Instead, she listened attentively as Catherine pulled back the curtain to reveal layers of a life that no one would believe about this woman sitting next to her unless she told them so herself. And Suzanne clung to the words that came straight from her friend's mouth and held onto them as though she were a starving woman being offered bread. Catherine did not just offer Suzanne a crumb, instead she set out a meal for Suzanne to feast upon.

It was hard to believe what she placed before her—forgiveness and love and hope—*all of this was being offered to her, for free.* She felt so unworthy, yet she was hungry for every morsel and devoured Catherine's words as she declared the truth about who God was and why He sent Christ to die for her.

Catherine continued, "You know, Suzanne, none of us are worthy. We don't earn our way into Heaven. We can't earn God's love. He loves us regardless of our behavior. His love is not based upon our performance but upon the simple fact that we belong to Him."

Catherine went on to say, "If we based our salvation on our feelings, we would only be saved on the days we feel good and what Jesus did for us would be for nothing. And, if we based our salvation on our good works, then we could earn it ourselves, and we would not need Jesus. *Our salvation is based on our faith in what Jesus did and not what we do. It's all because of grace.*"

Suzanne held on to every single sentence as she sat crying in their booth while silverware and dishes clattered in the distance and nearby patrons talked and laughed about nothing as serious or heartbreaking as what they were sharing. Ironically, the banana bread she ordered was untouched along with her coffee but the real bread she was offered was something that would last her the rest of her life.[17]

They talked a little more, then she thanked Catherine for listening and sharing God's truth with her. Catherine was a wise woman. They paid the bill and rose from their seats. She hugged Catherine and whispered, "Thank you for your special friendship to me, thank you for not judging me." She squeezed her hand and said, "Pray for me." Together they walked to the parking lot and said goodbye.

Suzanne knew what she needed to do. She drove home from the restaurant, walked into her house that just a couple of hours ago seemed like a dark and lonely prison, full of voices tormenting and taunting her, and knelt beside her bed. She cried and cried. She asked God to forgive her for her sin, she told Him how sorry she was.

She asked Him to help her understand how He could forgive her, because it was a mystery to her how God could forgive or love her in spite of her sin. She thanked Him for loving her even though she abandoned Him, and she remained kneeling by her bed for a very long time crying and repenting. When she rose, she possessed an indescribable peace. She knew she was forgiven. She knew she had communed with God and truly touched Him, and He loved her and forgave her.

She then opened her Bible, turning to a passage in the book of John. She felt like a hundred pounds were lifted off her when her eyes fell upon John 8:10-11:

"Then Jesus stood up again and said to the woman, 'Where are your accusers? Didn't even one of them condemn you?' 'No, Lord,' she said. And Jesus said, 'Neither do I.'"

The next day at church, Catherine approached Suzanne and handed her what looked to be a letter. But inside the envelope was just a sheet of paper with Scriptures written on it which turned out to be just what Suzanne would need in the future because Satan does not just give up on accusing.

She learned to fight when she heard the voices in her head—*because they weren't gone*—so she would read over it, sometimes even out loud. The accusations came at times when she was weak or not thinking about it. The verse she clung to the most was "there is no condemnation to those who are in Christ Jesus."[18]

She knew where the voices were coming from. She had been taught for many years that Satan is the "accuser of the brethren" and that all his demons are constantly warring against the people of God.[19] Then she was reminded of the Scripture in Ephesians that says we are not fighting against flesh and blood, but principalities and powers of darkness and wickedness in high places.[20] And when she heard those voices say, "You are not a Christian" or "You are a murderer," she would answer them with God's word and remind herself of what God says about His forgiveness, His love and His acceptance of her.

She knew she was forgiven because there was a reassurance within her placed there by Holy Spirit.

But the paper with the Scriptures on it that Catherine gave her helped her fight this battle of feeling unworthy and unacceptable. She kept it close and read the Scriptures written on it many times when she needed to be reminded what God's Word says about confessing your sin and the forgiveness He offers.

The Scriptures she read were:

If we confess our sins, he is faithful and just and will forgive us our sins and purify us from all unrighteousness. 1 John 1:9, NIV

Through Christ, you are acceptable to God, holy and blameless without a single fault. Colossians 1:22, paraphrased

Therefore, there is now no condemnation for those who are in Christ Jesus. Romans 8:1, NIV

Purify me from my sins, and I will be clean; wash me, and I will be whiter than snow. Oh, give me back my joy again; you have broken me—now let me rejoice. Don't keep looking at my sins. Remove the stain of my guilt. Create in me a clean heart, O God. Renew a loyal spirit within me. Psalms 51:7-10

He has removed our sins as far from us as the east is from the west. Psalms 103:12

Unfortunately, it was a very long time before Suzanne could really begin to understand the depth of God's forgiveness because every time she looked at Erin, she saw the pain all over her face.

Michael
1992-1995

Michael came home to visit his parents all through his college years. When they attended church together on Sunday morning, he would sometimes see Erin there with her previously elusive mother. She actually looked like a pretty nice lady to him. He still didn't understand all of that. And he wondered if she knew who he was.

Sometimes, he would see Erin's mother looking at him funny and it bugged him. Did she know? Erin was still beautiful, but she looked so different now, her eyes held an emptiness about them that gave him an eerie feeling. He always felt guilty. She dressed a lot differently than when they dated. He never spoke to her, nor did she speak to him. They would look the other way if they saw one another. Eventually, he stopped attending that church and moved away. It was such a relief to not to have to see Erin regularly anymore.

CHAPTER 11

New Beginnings

Now you are the body of Christ,
and each one of you is a part of it.
1 Corinthians 12:27, NIV

Erin

1995-2001

Erin finished high school. She worked through the summer and began classes in the autumn at Atlanta Tech. She and her mother never talked about that day again. Her mother tried but Erin refused. A few months after the abortion, her mom asked her to lunch on a Saturday; she chose a place where they could talk quietly without being overheard. She conveyed to Erin that she had wanted to talk to her a very long time now about what happened back then and she apologized to her for not coming to her sooner. She touched Erin's hand and asked her to please listen to what she needed to say. When Erin realized what their meeting was going to be about, she instinctively pulled away from her mother. She almost left the table because she did not want to go there with her mother or anyone else for that matter. But instead, she listened to her mother confess to her how wrong she had been. Suzanne acknowledged to Erin that she made the biggest mistake of her life—a mistake that changed both of their lives forever. As she shared with Erin all the dark days that followed, Erin thought about all of her dark days that preceded and followed that day. Her mother confessed to Erin that she knew she wrongly advised and pressured her to abort her child and she now knew the abortion had wounded Erin so very deeply. She confessed to Erin that she knew she coerced her to do something she did not want to do, murder a child, Erin's child, and her first grandchild. She then confessed to Erin that months ago she asked God to forgive her and stated confidently that she knew He forgave her; but now she needed to ask Erin to forgive her. She broke down and cried in front of Erin and, surprisingly, Erin enjoyed watching her mother suffer. She thought back to all her pain and all she suffered—and still was suffering.

Granted, her mom did seem sincere and the feelings she expressed to her about all that transpired a few months ago seemed genuine, but her words were pointless to Erin. Inside she silently screamed, *Seriously? You are the Christian, you are my mother, and you did something to me for which I will never be able to forgive you. You pressured me to kill my child!*

Yet, she couldn't help but think that she did the same thing just a couple of years ago that her mom was completely clueless about. And, she corrected her mother in her thoughts, it wasn't her first grandchild—it was her second. Moreover, it was ultimately her decision the second time, too.

Nonetheless, to keep the peace so her mom wouldn't freak out or make a scene and start crying uncontrollably, or worse yet, possibly not pay for her to go to college, she replied in a distant tone, "Sure, Mom, I forgive you." Yet Erin remained chained to her silent prison of sadness, regret and shame.

Suzanne was so grateful to hear Erin say she forgave her; immediately she felt a heaviness lift off her. She tried to be as honest with Erin as best as she knew how, but she felt that this conversation was not fruitful. She perceived that Erin was still not ready to *talk* about any of it. Sadly, she sensed Erin was still shut down toward her emotionally and the wall that existed between them for so long since Paul's death remained. Yet, simply hearing her say she forgave her gave Suzanne hope that one day they would be able to talk and possibly grow close again. It was the desire of her heart and she would continue to hope and pray for it.

Erin's pain was all bottled up inside her. All the bitterness she felt for Michael, Joe, her mom, and God would never go away. All the ill feelings she felt about herself were still there too.

Erin worked as often as she could on Sundays to give herself an excuse not to attend church. Church was something that she didn't get anymore. She used to love church when her dad was alive. They would go together as a family and then go out to lunch afterwards. She liked the praise music, the Bible stories and the friends she made. But she'd been a little girl then, and after her dad died and her mom stopped going, she stopped missing it. When her mom was totally out of it, she'd gone a few times with her friend Christy, even hoping her mom would begin taking her again one day; but that didn't happen.

And later, when her mom finally *got it together*, she'd made Erin go back to church with her. Even then, it was okay—up until her mom made her go to that clinic. She knew her mom didn't know about the first abortion; she couldn't hold that against her. She would always blame Michael for that and *her stupidity about boys*. She couldn't believe she wanted to marry him at age fifteen. What was she thinking?

Yet, when it happened again with Joe, and she confided to her mom and asked her, no *begged her*, to let her keep her baby. Her *super Christian mom* refused, or let her know she wouldn't help her, that she would be out on her own. Basically, she offered abortion to her as her only way out, made the appointment and paid for it. Erin was shocked that her mother could do something like that. Erin did not think much of her after that, nor her religion, or her God.

That day changed everything for Erin and what she thought about her mom and everyone else up to that point at that place they called a church—*they were simply hypocrites.*

When Erin thought about it, Michael was a churchgoer too. She even saw him at church a couple of times when he was home from college. She always avoided him as he did her. All of these people in her life were just liars and hypocrites. What did it even mean to say you were a Christian? She would always think, *Yeah, right ...*

Christy was okay though. She said she was a Christian and she never really let Erin down but she also didn't push anything down her throat. Christy's mom, Catherine, was okay too. She was consistently nice to her. And Joe? Well, he never went to church so he was the only authentic one out of the bunch. He never told her he was anything. He just didn't want a baby. But he was still a jerk.

So, despite everything, her dad's death, the two lousy boyfriends, the two trips to the abortion clinic and all the pain after, Erin graduated high school, started college at a tech school and made good grades. Later she transferred to a state college. She lived at home for the first two years and concentrated on doing well so she could join her friend Christy at a state college. It certainly had not been easy, and now, she was finally able to get away from all these fake people. Erin was more than pleased about that.

After Erin transferred and then graduated with a degree in business in May of 1998, she began working for her father's friend, Jim, who promised her a job all those years ago. He was true to his promise; that meant a lot to Erin. He owned lots of storefront properties and needed a manager to help negotiate his leases to fill the commercial spaces, serve the community and not allow similar businesses to compete with one another.

Erin was twenty-two when she began working for her dad's old friend. Jim treated her as an adult and a professional which made her extremely happy. He had been fond of her dad. When he talked with Erin about him, Jim would reflect on how shocked he was when he heard about the accident. He would always shake his head and say, "He was one heck of a nice guy." It pleased Erin to have an employer who previously knew her Daddy. She still missed him so much—does that ever go away, the missing of someone you loved dearly? Sadly, Erin covered her pain with layers of bitterness. She was a walking emotional wreck, but she functioned very well to hide her scars. In fact, she was so good at pretending, she became a perfectionist.

Erin felt she had lost control in so many areas of her life. Her father died. She knew she could not have controlled that. She could not undo the past about the abortions; that was in the past. What she realized now was she could control her job and her future, so she worked very hard at being excellent at what she did—*and she was*. Erin dated very little. She had been wounded and hurt by two males and wasn't excited about the next one she would meet. When she thought about Michael and Joe, she thought about the babies and the pain and the guilt. She wondered whether they would have been a boy or a girl? Erin kept up with their ages—if they'd lived. She went so far as to wonder what color their hair or eyes would have been.

She secured her first apartment; really, it was just a studio, but she was finally on her own. She earned a degree, landed a job, *and was finally away from her mother, her church and all those fake Christians.*

Emotionally, she was broken and bruised. She didn't let herself get close to anyone because, truthfully, she didn't trust anyone.

But things changed because one day Erin met a man. His name was John. He came to inquire about a commercial space for his insurance business. She was now twenty-four; he was thirty-two. He was married briefly out of college but it had ended in divorce when his wife cheated on him. He was hurt deeply and was looking for someone he could trust. He did not have any children and was very careful about whom he dated.

Erin was so careful about men that she seemed frozen. She'd built so many walls around herself that when John met her, he wondered if she was already in a relationship or maybe even married, though she wore no ring. He noticed she wore a locket around her neck and wondered about it. Erin noticed John from the very first time they met and watched him carefully, possibly a bit more than other clients who were semi-attractive in their business suits and fancy cars. She dressed very professionally in pencil skirts and tailored jackets because she wanted to portray a successful image to the business owners with whom she dealt. Frankly, she wanted her boss to approve of her. He was the closest person to being a father figure.

John was attracted to Erin immediately. She was a beautiful girl, tall and lean, with dark blonde hair and beautiful bright blue eyes. He studied and scrutinized her each time they met to go over his lease. As they negotiated it, he would try to learn a little bit more about her each time. It wasn't easy to get to know her. He felt there was an awkwardness. Sometimes, he would make up excuses to come by her office to ask a dumb question just so he could see her. He wasn't sure if she would even want to go out with him, so he left it alone for a while.

But one day, Erin let her guard down and she actually flirted with John a little bit, teasing him about negotiating his lease so economically so he could hold on to his money for what?

She pointed out that he obviously didn't have a girlfriend to spend it on, and then she giggled. So, he decided that day that she was simply a girl who needed to be *handled with care*.

There was a final meeting in Erin's office to finish up his lease. As they sat hunched over the paperwork, almost touching, going over details John needed to close this deal, neither noticed the time. It was after 7 p.m. They were both happy that the deal was done.

John, very nonchalantly, invited her out to dinner to celebrate their successful negotiation as well as his new beginning in this new location. Because Erin was hungry, she accepted. She wasn't even sure why. Sure, she liked him, but mostly, she felt good around him. She could not remember having this feeling for a very long time. Only time would tell if she could trust him.

The way he negotiated the lease was admirable. She could tell he was honest and forthright. She personally thought he was someone who had a lot of integrity. *He seemed to be that guy who would do the right thing when no one was looking.* They talked a little about his insurance business. She even shared with him her mother's troubles with life insurance after her father died. He seemed genuinely sorry for what her mother went through as well as what she experienced, being so young when she'd lost her father.

Erin thought John was attractive and liked the fact that he was a bit older. She wondered if he was married when they'd first met. Somewhere in one of their conversations, it came up, and he confided to her that he was previously, but he was now divorced. John did not elaborate. He didn't seem to want to talk about his past. Erin certainly didn't want to talk about her past. So, they went out that evening and enjoyed themselves. They talked openly and honestly. Erin did not get home until after 11 p.m. that night. Soon, they were going to lunches and more dinners.

After they dated for several months, Erin confided to John many things about her life as well as her viewpoints on things. She discussed with him how she felt about Christians and opened up to him about how hypocritical she thought they were. She even told him about both her abortions and the circumstances surrounding them. He grieved with her over the abortions. She told him that she was not sure if she could conceive a child if she ever did marry one day because of the many things she read about abortion and the damage it causes to young women for future pregnancies.

Then 9/11 struck America and the nation was forever changed. September 11 shook everyone up and overnight people became much more serious about their country, their faith and their family. Erin had recently celebrated her twenty-fifth birthday. She and John were close, but after this tragedy, they became even closer. People began to treat each other nicer and the overall climate changed everywhere. People began talking more about God, and they began going back to church and there was a measure of fear too.

Erin became afraid that something awful would happen in her city of Atlanta, that it would be targeted because of its size. She began to lean more on John. Erin came to realization that she wanted and needed someone in her life.

There was this one thing though, John was a Christian, and Erin still had a major problem with Christians. She remembered how much she thought she loved Jesus back before her daddy died and even afterward she prayed and asked God to help her through the pain. But after what happened with Michael and then her perfect Christian mother, she gave up entirely on God and so-called Christians. Whenever she heard anyone talking about Christianity or anything associated with it, she just turned her emotions off and thought, *These people are deluded.* Still, she had to admit, John seemed different.

John was not secretive about his belief in God, but he was cautious and waited until he felt comfortable sharing with Erin. One day, he finally talked to Erin about his faith. He told her what being a Christian meant to him. He explained to her about grace and forgiveness. He shared with her how no one is righteous[21], and how he was not relying on his performance to save him—but the blood of Christ. He helped Erin to see that everyone sins and that Christianity does not exempt you from sinning, it just gives you hope for eternity. He added, "When we sin, the Holy Spirit is there to convict us of our sin and to help us get back on the right path." Erin began to see Christianity through John's eyes. Things were a bit different after that.

John invited her to his church where she began to understand much more about God's nature and character. She began to realize that there are no perfect Christians; they are simply forgiven. She grasped the fact that no matter how hard she would try, she could not live up to God's standard of perfection *and neither could her mother*. Things began to make a little more sense to her.

One Sunday, Erin prayed the sinner's prayer at the end of the service. She left church that day feeling freer than she'd been in a very long time. She realized she needed forgiveness and once she received it, she began to feel a peace and even an acceptance for others in her heart.

She continued going to church with John, all the while kicking around her very sincere questions about God and Christians and things in general. John would always try to answer as best he could, usually getting out his Bible. Erin began to understand more and more about the Christian faith. John clearly did not know everything, and he was quick to point that out. He shared with Erin some things he did understand and urged her to look for answers on her own, too. He said that faith is a journey and the more we immerse ourselves in the Word of God, the more God will be revealed to us. The most important thing was Erin held the assurance that she was forgiven by God through the blood of Christ, not by anything she had done or could do. She was so thankful for this gift of salvation.

She realized, upon her confession of faith, that the only work required was to trust in Jesus alone for her salvation. Her gratitude often moved her to tears of joy. She believed in the Redeemer God sent.[22] Erin finally found the peace that surpasses all understanding[23] … a peace that filled the haunting void that was missing in her life for so very long.

They soon considered themselves a couple and went out regularly. She talked with John about her past—how she resented her mother and how she still was not able to completely let it go. After listening to the whole story, John agreed that her mother had sinned but once she saw how wrong she was, she handled it correctly by taking it to God and then asking Erin to forgive her. "After all," he'd said, "What else could she do?"

He then talked with Erin about her own sin both times she went to the clinic and aborted her children. John told her that even though there was a boy involved the first time and her mother the second time who put pressure on her and coerced her, she still was responsible for her part in both decisions. She needed to be cleansed to remove the weight of the sin she carried all these years.

Erin listened to all John said. One night soon after their conversation, in the privacy of her bedroom, Erin asked God to forgive her for aborting her two children. Once she did, she felt so much better, she felt clean and the heavy weight she carried was gone. She received God's forgivenesss. The one thing she did not do was talk to her mother about either abortion, the secret one nor the one her mom was involved in. However, she did share with her that she'd ask Christ into her life.

After months of dating and getting to know each other, Erin and John fell in love. He proposed to her on Christmas Eve of 2001 as they walked in the beautiful Atlanta Botanical Gardens. Yet, instead of marrying right away, they decided to wait. They did not set a date for a wedding because neither of them wanted to rush into anything. And most importantly, they both decided to abstain from sex until they were married. Erin was still living with the lesson that comes from the emotional pain of premarital sex, and John quickly agreed, though it was hard.

It was time well spent. A little over a year later, on Valentine's Day of 2003, when Erin was twenty-six and John was thirty-four, she walked down the aisle of the church where they both now attended. Erin was escorted by her employer, Jim, her daddy's friend, whom she had become close to over the years. She wore a beautiful ivory vintage gown with a chapel train. It was a modest A-line gown with a plunging sweetheart neckline. Ivory lace overlaid the entire dress. There were pearl buttons all the way down the back of the dress. She was accompanied by two attendants, Christy and a college friend, Amy. They each wore a purple satin, floor-length simple design. The bouquets they held consisted of pink sweetheart roses and baby's breath and were trimmed with purple ribbons. Erin carried a simple bouquet consisting of white roses, accented with greenery and baby's breath, trimmed in an ivory lace ribbon.

The ceremony was simple and beautiful. It was an evening service with just a few friends and family. Candles were placed all around the perimeter of the dimly lit church, and, as they flickered, it created an illusion of mystique and romance. But there was something more and far more precious: the atmosphere was of a *holy* union between a man and his beloved.

When John gazed at Erin as she walked down the aisle toward him, she seemed to glow in her beautiful dress. When their eyes met, his eyes welled up with tears, and he knew that he was blessed that day. God was giving him a second chance at love.

Erin, on the other hand, restrained herself and held her thoughts very close to her heart; she could not even begin to let one tear fall because if she had, they would have never ended due to all the gratitude she felt for God and John and the chance at a new beginning. It was something too precious and too deep to be expressed in words.

Michael
1995-2001

Michael graduated from college in May of 1995 and was accepted to law school at Auburn University. In 1998, when he finished and passed the bar, he joined a large Atlanta law firm at an entry level position. His plan was to eventually set up his own practice, but for now, he wanted to train with a good firm and become proficient in corporate law. He soon began dating a girl named Julie who worked in his office building as a paralegal. Julie was from Florida and attended and graduated from Emory College. She decided to stay in Atlanta—a city she grew to love.

They began going out and spending a lot of time together. They would talk about law with one another and enjoyed picking each other's brains about the little technicalities. He would stay over at her place some nights and she at his apartment as well. They were sexually active, but Michael always made sure he used a condom until he found out Julie was on the pill.

Soon, they became more serious and wanted to settle down and begin a family. So, in the fall of 2001, they married in Florida where Julie's parents still resided. They planned a beautiful beach destination wedding at a five-star resort. When the long weekend was over and some of the remaining guests were beginning to leave on Tuesday morning, September 11th, the twin towers were hit causing a major nightmare for all air travelers.

Thankfully, Michael and Julie left for Cabos on Sunday morning after their big Saturday night event. The tragic event did not affect them until it was time to come home, other than being preoccupied with the news and keeping abreast of the tragedy in New York City. Their flight back was delayed and rescheduled because of all the craziness surrounding the terrorist attacks.

Back in Atlanta, they settled down in a little condo and soon began attending church. Michael and Julie both came from faith-based backgrounds and 9/11 caused them to begin thinking about their roots. They discussed it and decided to go back to church and start fresh.

Within just a couple of months of their marriage, together they walked down to the front of their church to recommit their lives to Christ. It was easy to do because half of the church was up there! So many people were fearful about what happened to the United States of America.

Soon thereafter, Julie began to dream of having a baby. In fact, she talked nonstop about starting a family. Michael began to think about it too, and got excited at the prospect of becoming a father one day.

Julie stopped taking the pill and soon became pregnant. They were both thrilled, but within weeks of finding out their news, Julie fell ill and ended up in the hospital with a ruptured fallopian tube. The doctors called it an ectopic pregnancy. Julie almost died from internal bleeding. Michael was horrified. The scare really shook him.

When the ER doctors asked Julie about her previous medical history, Michael found out that Julie had an abortion when she was nineteen, long before they met. She never told him much about her past, so it surprised him and he was even a little upset about it at first. Deep down, it bothered him because he thought she was better than that—*and then he remembered Erin*.

Julie lost one of her fallopian tubes. The doctor told her she could still become pregnant, though it may take a little longer.

After three years passed, Julie realized the ectopic pregnancy scarred her in more ways than one. Michael knew his wife was suffering emotionally, and he felt bad for her. At times, he thought about Erin, wondering if his coercing her to have an abortion had caused her any emotional or physical harm.

One day, Julie came home from work and told Michael that she felt the need to get some counseling to help her move past her abortion as well as the loss of their baby. She said she realized she had never dealt with it. *Dealt with it?* he thought, *It was over … in the past,* but he told Julie to do whatever she needed to do. She began going to some post abortion classes at a pregnancy support center which someone from their church mentioned to her.

After several weeks of classes, Michael noted Julie's transformation and the freedom she found. Julie shared with Michael that she realized not only did she need to receive forgiveness for herself *but she also needed to forgive herself*. And she did.

As she learned each week, Julie shared those truths with Michael. He could see that she possessed an inner peace, a deep, abiding serenity. Michael was confused about all of it because he believed it was in the irretrievable past. Yet, every now and then, a wave of guilt swept over him when he allowed himself to think about Erin.

Forgiving, Trusting and Healing

If we confess our sins,
He is faithful and just
and will forgive us our sins and
purify us from all unrighteousness.
1 John 1:9, NIV

Suzanne and Erin
2004

Erin and John settled in to their new married life. The only thing missing for them was a child. They hoped and prayed that God would bless them with a baby to complete their union. Since their honeymoon just six months ago, they were desperately trying to have a child. And their faith, rather than diminishing, grew. They were deeply in love and committed to each other. Both decided that no matter what happened—*whether or not God chose to bless them with a child*—they would trust Him and not allow themselves to become bitter. They surrendered their will to His and lived and grew closer to each other.

And then, it happened in the seventh month of their marriage. Erin and John conceived a child. They were elated. Yet, eight weeks into the pregnancy, Erin miscarried. She felt like a failure as a wife and more than anything, she felt that God was punishing her for everything that happened before. She thought to herself, *Why would God allow me to have a child when I killed two?* She thought of the Scripture that said, "Children are a gift from God"[24] and what had she done with those gifts? She killed them.

Erin's mother, Suzanne, was delighted about the pregnancy. She purchased a layette and gift wrapped it for Erin and John. It contained an all-white, organic cotton blanket trimmed in white satin, several little white onesies, a couple of white crib sheets, little tiny white wash-cloths and soft white knitted booties. Suzanne thought it was all so delicate and lovely. She added a little white lamb and presented it to Erin and John on Christmas along with their other gifts. Erin was only six weeks along then. Sadly, just two weeks later, they let her know about Erin's miscarriage.

Almost a year passed, and Erin began to face the cold hard realization that possibly she would never have a child. The children she'd aborted were the children God planned to give her; yet she destroyed them. She couldn't let go of the nagging thought that maybe God was still punishing her, even though she knew she'd asked for forgiveness and was assured through Scripture that she was forgiven.

She talked to John about it at times. He always would point her to the truth of what God's Word says, but she kept hearing the words, "Consequences of sin" rolling around in her brain.

If that weren't enough, it seemed that every time Erin saw her mother, she would feel all kinds of negative emotions toward her. The bitterness would well up inside her. Erin found herself reliving that day her mom took her to the clinic and the day at lunch months later when her mom cried and asked Erin to forgive her. Erin went through the motions; she nodded and told her mother, "Yes, I forgive you," *but deep down inside Erin had not forgiven her*. Now, every time she saw her mother, she would fantasize about the child that was gone.

She would think about how old he or she would be. She would have a ten-year-old little boy or girl if it were not for her mother pressuring her to abort. And, she thought guiltily, she would have a twelve-year-old, too.

The feelings continued to nag Erin. They began to interfere with her prayer life. Also, each time she took a pregnancy test, which was much too often because of her erratic periods and also because she was so hopeful, her mother's face would consistently appear before her, followed by Michael's and Joe's. Erin would become so confused; tears came easily. Erin began to face the reality that she was still holding on to unresolved anger. *The bitterness continued to linger in the air like the smell of her morning coffee.*

The days sped by and blended into weeks and then months. One morning, Erin was so hopeful that this would be the day the test would show up positive;

her period was several days late. She even convinced herself that she was having morning sickness upon rising. She believed her prayers would be answered today. However, she received a negative reading *and when she saw the minus sign—again, her mother's face appeared before her*. This time Erin broke down and cried. Her shoulders shook with despair as she poured out her heart to the Lord. Erin asked God to help her find a way to forgive her mother.

She met John later because they made dinner reservations at their favorite restaurant hoping for a special dinner. Instead of celebrating a pregnancy that night, Erin talked with John, confiding in him about her bitterness toward her mother. John was supportive and told her not to be too hard on herself. He'd told her how we are all human with human emotions. Yet, he warned Erin about her unforgiveness and shared with her how it was connected to our own forgiveness. John seemed to always be able to help Erin each time she struggled with her faith, He would point her to answers. She was so thankful for him. He led her to the Scripture in Matthew that talks about unforgiveness:

> *But if you refuse to forgive others, your Father will not forgive your sins.* Matthew 6:15

The dinner turned out to be a celebration after all because Erin was finally able to let it all go. Later that night, as she lay in her bed after reading her Bible and thinking about it some more, she confessed her unforgiveness as she wept. As she lay on her back praying, tears rolled out of the corners of her eyes and down past her temples dampening her hair. She lay there basking in God's unconditional love and forgiveness as John lay sleeping peacefully beside her.

The next day was Saturday and so she called her mother and asked if they could meet for coffee. They agreed on a Starbucks because they were now popping up everywhere. One was located conveniently between their two homes.

It was early May and spring was in the air, so after ordering their coffees, they walked outside. The sun was shining in the clear blue sky, and they began to look for a place to sit. Erin cupping her favorite concoction, a skinny mocha latte, and Suzanne sticking with plain black coffee but adding lots of half and half, settled themselves at a table for two. It felt good to bask in the warmth of the sun and coffee—life's simple pleasures.

After catching up on regular news, Erin, now a much more mature woman of twenty-eight as opposed to the seventeen-year-old who sat talking with her mother all those years ago, began to confess her reason for wanting to meet. Erin shared with her mother all her thoughts and feelings. She told her how she hated her after the abortion, and how she never truly forgave her. Her mother listened and cried as Erin shared. Erin could see it was very painful for her mother to relive that day, just as it was for her.

As they shared their hearts with one another, Erin began to realize just how human her mother was. Erin listened as her mother shared with her *how she too struggled with her own faith* after Paul died and then again when she coerced Erin to abort her child.

Erin then confessed to her mother how desperate she was to now have a child. Suzanne, still feeling responsible for Erin's fate, confessed to Erin how she prayed and prayed for her to be blessed with a child. Then they prayed together that one day, somehow, God would answer both their prayers.

Erin listened to her mother but she was so afraid to hope; yet she was also afraid not to hope. She was in a very strange place spiritually. She never mentioned the earlier abortion to her mother. *She simply could not go there.*

When they rose from the table that morning, Erin met her mother's eyes and held her gaze. She said, "Mom, I forgive you, none of us are perfect. I was seeking perfection in you, and I realize there is only one perfect person who ever lived and that is Jesus Christ."

Suzanne cried again. She hugged Erin and then she thanked Erin for her honesty; she promised Erin that she would continue to pray for her to have a successful pregnancy. When she left that day she was finally free of all the guilt and the condemnation she always knew Erin carried around toward her.

Suzanne thanked God for His sovereign role in all of it. *Over ten years had passed and now it was time to let it all go.*

A Gift From God

*Children are a gift from the Lord;
they are a reward from him.*

Psalms 127:3

Erin, John and Jonathan

November 10, 2005

On November 10, 2005, John and Erin welcomed Jonathan Paul into the world.

He was the most beautiful baby she ever saw. Suzanne cried and cried when Erin presented the little bundle of joy to her mother with tears in her own eyes.

She whispered to her, "Thank you for your prayers, I never thought I would see this day." John beamed and cried too. He whispered over and over each time he held his newborn son "What a miracle, just look at him."

Erin's friend, Christy, now married, had recently found out she was pregnant and could not wait to hold Jonathan in her arms as she thought about what was to come for her in just a few months.

Christy's mom, Catherine, came to the hospital as well. She stood off to the side smiling, eyes shining with tears with a knowing look on her face.

All the past pain of Erin's life was erased in one single second when she peeked down on this precious baby boy whom she named Jonathan Paul—Jonathan after her husband, and Paul after her daddy.

She carefully researched the meaning of names and was thrilled to find that Jonathan meant a "gift from God." And he truly was. Up until this very moment, Erin did not know if God truly forgave her. But now, as she held her little newborn baby—her son, in her arms, *she knew God was a loving God. He had forgiven her. He loved her. He made Her complete in motherhood.*

She was tired from the labor but the feeling of happiness overwhelmed her. She could not think of anything other than—*all is right with the world*. She was twenty-nine years old. It was fourteen years ago that fifteen-year-old Erin took matters into her hands and made the mistake that would scar her forever.

She saw that God truly does give second chances and third ones and fourth and fifth … the chances never stop coming because His love and His faithfulness never stop … and no matter what happens God is a God who loves us and is pulling for us and He wants to bless us. *He never abandoned me; He was always there; I just didn't know it then,* were her thoughts as she drifted into a much-needed, deep sleep.

Michael and Julie
2004-2008

Four years after Michael and Julie were married, they were finally able to have a successful pregnancy. Julie gave birth to a baby boy.

Michael could not believe it. He was so amazed by all of it. Julie told Michael from the very beginning when their baby's heart began beating—just 21 days into her pregnancy. Each week she would relay facts to Michael about how big their baby was compared to things like oranges and melons. She would share with Michael which parts of their baby were forming.

Michael would always think, *Wow, there's a baby in there! My baby!* And every single thing that happened in the womb from then on was shared with Michael from when the baby started growing hair, forming teeth, growing fingernails and even when he hiccupped. And Michael witnessed Julie's belly growing as well as her discomfort. When the baby would kick or move, he was fascinated with the life inside her. Upon the birth of his child, Michael was absolutely amazed and awe struck at this new life. When he saw his son for the first time, whom they named Michael Allen Junior, he was hypnotized with wonder at the complete formation from his tiny toes and fingers to how he slept and cried. Michael was also fascinated as he witnessed the beginnings of his sweet little personality.

Julie went through ten hours of labor but she was determined to make it without a C-section. The last two hours were very hard labor. Though she was tired and spent from pushing, sweating and groaning, anyone could see the contentment and joy all over her face when she held baby Michael in her arms for the first time.

A couple of years later, when little Michael was around two, Michael took him to play in the park. Time after time he would help his little boy up when he fell down. After becoming a father, his own faith began to grow, and he began to ponder the love a father has for his children. He thought there was nothing this little guy could do that would make him stop loving him, and no matter what kind of a jam this little fella could ever get himself into, he would want to be there for him. He would move Heaven and earth to make things right for his child. And for some reason, he began to think about his past. He began thinking about Erin and what all he did to her. He became overwhelmed with grief for that entire situation and, at the same time, he realized he took part in the murder of his first child. Michael realized that he hurt a girl who had already lost her father. She was so vulnerable and he selfishly took advantage of her. As he thought about this, to his surprise, he began to cry.

A year later, when Michael and Julie were expecting their second child, Michael could not handle the pain of his unconfessed sin any longer. He finally talked to Julie about it. She proved to be more than understanding because of her past and the counseling she received. She couldn't help but ask him why he made her feel so bad about her past when he owned a similar one as well. After many tears and hugs, she urged Michael to see one of the associate pastors in their church.

While at the counseling appointment, Michael simply laid everything out on the table. The Pastor and he talked about his youth, the mistakes and God's path of forgiveness. Through counsel, it did not take Michael long to realize what was needed. The main thing that was conveyed to Michael through his Pastor was that God is a God of grace, mercy and forgiveness. Michael was already sorry; he simply needed to confess his sin to God, come clean and ask for forgiveness. It was there waiting for him all along. It was so strange to him when he realized how long he'd carried around this burden, it was years, and in just one prayer, he was totally free.

This Pastor then shared a story that Michael was familiar with about King David in the Bible. King David lusted after a married woman named Bathsheba, and summoned her to his chambers while her husband was off fighting a war for Israel. When she became pregnant, instead of being truthful about it, he ordered her husband killed, a man who was one of David's mightiest and most honored warriors. The Pastor continued to share how David repented and received God's forgiveness and found peace within. Yet the illegitimate child became sick and died even though David prayed for him to recover. Later, God blessed David and Bathsheba with a child who grew up to be King Solomon. So, this story showed Michael how God truly does forgive and how God allows for second chances. God continues to love you no matter what and will never ever turn his back on you. He is a God of redemption—He can bring good out of any bad situation.

Michael could not help but think about his son and how he would do anything for him. The Pastor talked to Michael about how God looks at our heart. God knows when we are genuinely sorry. All we have to do is ask and He is ready and willing to forgive us. Michael left that day free from all the pain and the guilt of his past.

Later, he read this Scripture in his Bible:

Oh, what joy for those
whose disobedience is forgiven,
whose sin is put out of sight!

Yes, what joy for those
whose record the Lord has cleared of guilt,
whose lives are lived in complete honesty!

When I refused to confess my sin,
my body wasted away,
and I groaned all day long.

Day and night your hand of discipline was
heavy on me.
My strength evaporated like water
in the summer heat.

Finally, I confessed all my sins to you
and stopped trying to hide my guilt.
I said to myself, "I will confess my rebellion to
the Lord."
And you forgave me! All my guilt is gone.

Psalms 32:1-5

The Familiar Girl

For now we see only a reflection as in a mirror;
then we shall see face to face.
Now I know in part; then I shall know fully,
even as I am fully known.
1 Corinthians 13:12, NIV

Suzanne

Heaven, Eternity A.D.

As Suzanne gazed upon this very familiar girl with interest, she noticed there were recognizable features about her that stood out. Suzanne thought she looked a lot like she did when she was young, yet, she could also see characteristics of Paul and Erin, and even her parents and grandparents.

"Hi," said the girl as she stood before Suzanne. "Hello," Suzanne responded. The familiarity of this girl at first confused Suzanne. She hesitated and started to ask, *Who are you?* But before she could finish her question, she knew exactly who this girl was. Everything that was once hidden was now revealed.[25] Before the question was formed, Suzanne was conscious of the knowledge of it. Nothing was hidden. Suzanne was aware that she was responsible for this girl's death. They equally understood it. But there was no hatred or condemnation from the girl, nor from anyone or anywhere. Only love exuded from this place. The girl smiled genuinely at Suzanne, and then she said. "I am so glad to meet you, let me show you around." They discussed the beauty of Heaven and interacted with the animals while admiring the flowers and the plants. The girl stooped down to smell a beautiful crimson flower that was so pleasing to the eye, one Suzanne had never seen before on earth. The girl touched the petals and gazed on its beauty momentarily.

The girl was pleasant and possessed a delightful demeanor. She held an innocence about her, much more so than anyone Suzanne ever met. She knew this girl arrived here in Heaven prior to what would have been her natural birth, somewhere between conception and nine months of a pregnancy.

Suzanne continued to be illuminated with the knowledge that came from the Holy Spirit that there was no grudge or judgment toward her from anywhere or anyone. And all these thoughts and information were unfolded and delivered to Suzanne as she realized *this girl simply loved her*. Suzanne stated, "You are Erin's child." "Yes," the girl answered, "I am. I came here from the womb. I never lived on earth except for the eight weeks that I existed in the womb." As she spoke, Suzanne reflected on the trip to the clinic with Erin and the abortion. It was very clear in her mind.

The girl continued, "I was given a purpose, it was designed by God Himself and assigned to me as my special gifts and talents—but all of it was unfulfilled."

As thoughts continued to flash through and linger in Suzanne's mind, she listened attentively. The girl continued speaking to her in a carefree tone, "God has more than just one purpose for a life when He creates it; one of mine was to help my mom bear the burden of caring for you these last two years. God puts desires in us when He creates us. He placed a desire in me to care for the sick. I would have become a nurse after you died.

God also placed a love in my heart for you stronger than even the love I would have for my mother. We were to have a special bond. You and I would have shared our love for flowers and plants." As she continued talking in a distant, yet thoughtful way, she touched the most beautiful rose bush. Her fingers lightly caressed the soft petals of a pink rose. "At first" she said, "I was created to simply bring you joy, to help you bear the loss of your husband, and even to fill the emptiness that would remain after Mom left for college and began her career. The joy I would have brought you was a gift God wanted to give you to help you heal from your loss—first as an infant, then as a toddler and finally as a young girl. God gave me the name, Joy. I would be twenty-two now if I'd been allowed to be born."

Suzanne reflected on her grandson Jonathan's birth and how excited she was when he was born. She remembered how secretly she wanted a granddaughter, and here she was, the granddaughter whom Suzanne insisted upon "getting rid of."

Joy continued, "When you became ill, I was meant to help care for you these last two years. You and I would have been very close, our relationship would have been exceptional and would have lasted until today. None of what God planned was fulfilled because of the abortion.

God's plan was thwarted. Things would have been different for my mom and for you if I was not destroyed in the womb. My purpose was created solely by God. When He creates something, He always has a unique purpose for it. Our relationship would have been unusually close. Mom and John would not have had the strain of caring for you and Jonathan. The anxiety of them both working and caring for you would have been lifted because of me. And later, you wouldn't have been so lonely. I was meant to be there for you. God knew the future and created me in my mother's womb to help care for you while at the same time giving you to me to love unconditionally all the way up until today when you died."

While she spoke, Suzanne noted how the girl kept calling Erin mom and how the girl was aware of everything that happened in the past as well as the present since the abortion happened and, additionally, what was supposed to happen—*if she'd lived*.

Suzanne began to think about the last two years and reflected upon her life and grieved as she remembered all the times she was so lonely.

She remembered how often she wished someone could have been in her life that would love her unconditionally and just be there to hang out with her, someone she could talk to and spend time with. She reflected on her illness and especially the last six months as she was cared for by strangers coming and going in her home.

She reflected on the financial problems Erin and John had as they tried to help her juggle all the bills. This beautiful girl standing in front of her would have changed all of that. Her granddaughter, whom Suzanne insisted on aborting, would have changed so many things.

She had a deep understanding of how it should have been, but still no judgment from the girl or even from herself. The very essence of this place was peace, forgiveness and love. *Yet, God was also showing her truth.*

At some point during all of this, a thought flashed in Suzanne's heart, then a question. She wanted to know if she must ask this girl for forgiveness, but as this thought materialized, she knew. Yet, the girl named Joy came and knelt in front of her, she took both of Suzanne's hands in hers and held them.

She then gazed into her eyes and said, "We are all God's creation. You are God's creation. God is love and you are here by the blood of Jesus. His blood covers everything. When I came here, I was taught all of God's principles and one thing I know is this—*There is no condemnation to those who are in Christ Jesus,*[26] and I do not condemn you either. You are free of everything here that would cause you to feel guilt or pain. Anyone or anything that would condemn you is nonexistent here."

Suzanne continued to take in the beauty of Heaven and all that surrounded her. She experienced new knowledge. Each time she pondered a question, it was answered. Her granddaughter delighted in her grandmother and all her reactions to the beauty of Heaven as she proceeded to show her around.

Joy then took Suzanne to meet a girl of around twelve and, again, Suzanne realized this was Erin's child whom she miscarried before she became pregnant with Jonathan. She was not aborted, and God knew her future would be here. Joy introduced the girl to Suzanne by saying, "This is my sister; her name is Patience." Suzanne was amazed at the difference in the souls of the inhabitants in Heaven.

As she learned about Patience, she knew that this was the soul that was miscarried when Erin and John wanted a child so badly. Patience's purpose was exactly as her name implied, to help Erin and John learn patience and to continue trusting in God so that He would indeed usher in the gift that He held in store for them, Jonathan. Patience was surrounded by docile animals and was at ease with every one of them.

Suzanne was amazed at all the knowledge she was acquiring here and continued to be approached by others she knew. More friends and family members greeted the two girls as though there was a friendship that existed for years. There was a union of understanding by all of them—*followed by peace, love and joy.*

Suzanne's granddaughter then stated very matter-of-factly to her, "There is a place Jesus has prepared for you. Patience and I are going to take you there now." Suzanne immediately thought of the Scripture where Jesus was talking to His disciples and said to them, "In my house are many mansions, if it were not so, I would not have told you. I go to prepare a place for you."[27]

Suzanne then looked expectantly at the girls and replied "I can't wait to see it."

CHAPTER 15

A Heavenly Appointment

*No eye has seen, no ear has heard,
and no mind has imagined
what God has prepared
for those who love him.*

1 Corinthians 2:9

Suzanne's unknown granddaughter
Eternity, A.D.

Suzanne and her two granddaughters, Joy and Patience, traveled along a beautiful path.

There was a coastline of white sand and beautiful shells that framed a body of water. The water was a beautiful cerulean blue, and Suzanne could hear waves lapping in the distance from the movement of the water. She saw three springs of water flowing up and out of that body of water and they looked to be dancing as they flowed together in unison toward the river of life. As the three of them continued along the sandy path, Suzanne saw a garden and a white fence covered with a beautiful vine. She then saw a trellis encompassed by a vine full of blooming flowers framing the entrance of a path.

They took the path and momentarily stopped walking as the three of them stood together in front of a beautiful, white cottage. It was so inviting and warm, a place unlike anything Suzanne ever dreamed of as she examined the surroundings, yet she knew if she could have dreamed it up—*this would be it.*

Standing by the gate tending the flowers was another girl Suzanne did not know. Again, she looked somewhat familiar but Suzanne knew she'd never seen her on earth. She looked at her other two granddaughters questioningly. And just then, everything began to fit together for Suzanne, because in Heaven, a question is always answered with the truth. Her granddaughter, Joy said, "This is my older sister, your other granddaughter. Her name is Faith."

The girl exuded a beauty about her that comforted and drew Suzanne in and when she smiled, her face lit up. Her eyes were bright blue, just like Erin's and she noticed her long blond hair was beautiful and mimicked Erin's. The girl hugged Suzanne and said, "I am so happy to meet you."

And then Suzanne just knew. All of her questions were answered. Erin was pregnant before at the young age of fifteen just after Paul died. When she'd been lying on the sofa grieving over Paul, her daughter was in trouble. Erin missed her daddy so much that she sought out male love and affection—*in a boy.*

It was all so clear to her now—why Erin wanted to have the baby so badly, and Suzanne coerced her to abort it. That's why she was wounded for so long and carried her grudge for so long. *There were two losses, not one.* Really, there were three, because of Erin's miscarriage. She realized so many things now. *All three of Erin's losses were standing in front of her.*

Suzanne continued to gaze at the three beautiful girls for a very long time as her thoughts sped by and knowledge continued to melt away any confusion she had, while at the same time, answering any questions that lingered in her mind.

Faith, the oldest of the three girls, was twenty-four years old. She began to explain her purpose to Suzanne. "My purpose was for a family who desperately wanted a child. God planned for me to be adopted. The family that God chose for me was a family who prayed a very long time to have a child. They wanted to adopt and when my mom became pregnant with me, if she had not aborted me, a providential meeting was planned with that couple along with my mom and you. If I were not aborted, this family would have adopted me, and I would have been a blessing to them that would have changed each one of their lives."

She continued, "The couple waiting to adopt would not have ended up divorcing because they would have the child they prayed and asked God for, and their faith would have become stronger. Instead, they used drugs and alcohol to numb their pain. The woman eventually lost her life from an overdose. My life would have united them as a family, and I would have been a special blessing to the entire family. The woman who would have been my grandmother had always wanted a little girl, and I was to be a gift from

God to her too. She would have helped her son and daughter-in-law raise me; she would have loved me deeply and cared for me. Her life would have been richer because of me. My place was not with my mom or you, but with them. I would not have known my mom or you. God's purpose for me was for that family. My name is Faith because my purpose was to help my adoptive parent's family keep their faith. Instead, they were torn apart."

Additionally, my mother, Erin, would not have lost her faith in God because bringing me life would have given her strength rather than caused her bitterness and unforgiveness. She would not have taken so long to come to faith in Christ and your relationship with her would not have suffered so much. In fact, my birth would have increased yours and her faith in spite of the hardship and shame.

Faith continued to explain to Suzanne, "A talent God gifted me with was interior design, I would have become an interior decorator. God has used me here in Heaven with my gifts and talents and I have been given many opportunities to help design dwelling places that are being prepared for other believers. I stay busy utilizing my gifts, but this … " she smiled and said as she waved her hands toward the home that was to be Suzanne's, "This was a special assignment." Faith continued speaking to Suzanne, "It has been such a blessing for me to be given the pleasure of designing and preparing your home. Would you like to go in and see what Jesus and I have been preparing for you?" Suzanne was still processing and gathering information. Now she paused and exclaimed, "Yes!"

She enjoyed and retained such an expectation of wonder and excitement.

Together, the four of them, Suzanne and her three granddaughters, walked through the little gate and down the sandy path much like the old beach house she used to go to with her grandparents. They walked up to the front porch where a wooden swing hung from the ceiling.

When she walked into the place that was prepared for her, Suzanne thought *it was like a beautiful dream coming true.* She noticed a huge picture window that looked out on the beautiful glassy blue water. She could see the three springs of water as they glistened in the light; she looked through the window and noticed the sand and the little fence with the beautiful flowers. She began to look around the room, recognizing some things. Her senses were roused by prior things that gave her pleasure. She noticed new things that were so unique and she knew, if she was given the opportunity, she would have picked each one because of the beauty in each and every thing stirred something deep inside her.

This special place consisted of all her favorite colors and, as she stood trying to take it all in, she turned to gaze into the eyes of the three beautiful girls. She whispered, "This is all so breathtaking, including you three!"

She thought about each one of these girls' lives and how they were all planned out in advance, yet human will and human choices changed the outcome. However, their lives weren't wasted because God redeems all things. Suzanne was in Heaven, but she was at a loss for words. And as Suzanne stood there and worshipped God in His awe-inspiring and infinite wisdom, this Scripture came to mind:

No eye has seen, no ear has heard, and no mind has imagined what God has prepared for those who love him. 1 Corinthians 2:9

She thought about God and His perfect plan for creation and soon she would be given her purpose now that she was in Heaven. She wondered just what that would be?

Reflections

*Very truly I tell you,
whoever hears my word and
believes in him who sent me
has eternal life and will not be judged
but has crossed over from death to life.*

John 5:24, NIV

Erin, John and Jonathan

Oakland Cemetery, January 3, 2016

Erin stood at the gravesite wearing a long black wool coat, yet she still shivered in the cold January air. She wore mittens and wrapped around her neck was the scarf her mother knit for her shortly before she died. Her husband, John, and their ten-year-old son, Jonathan, stood beside her as they silently watched the casket containing her mother's body being lowered into the newly dug grave.

Erin's faith told her that her mother wasn't dead, only her body. Her faith told her that her mother was in Heaven. But was she? *She wondered what really happens when you die and what one would experience when they died.*

Erin hoped that everything she understood about eternal life was true. She believed that it was; that's what faith is, the substance of things hoped for, the evidence of things not seen.[28] And as she pondered Heaven and what it might be like, she thought how amazed her mother must be as she would soon be introduced to all three of her babies. *I guess she'll be surprised,* she thought.

Her husband, John, stood next to her; she took his hand in hers along with their son, Jonathan's, and squeezed them both tightly. "Let's go," she said. "Grandma isn't here; it's only her body."

EPILOGUE

Therefore, angels are only servants—
spirits sent to care for people
who will inherit salvation.
Hebrews 1:14

Suzanne, her angel and the little girl
Heaven, Outside Time

Suzanne ventured down a tree-lined path and, as the light filtered through the towering trees, she reflected on the mission that was given to her upon her arrival in Heaven. As she focused on God's plan for her, she remained overwhelmed and astounded at His love and His unique plan for all of creation.

Suzanne interacted with many other inhabitants in Heaven including her three granddaughters, her family and friends. Even though Heaven was outside of time, souls arrived continuously in intervals. Some she knew on earth and some she didn't … but once here, strangers they were not. And she met those who inspired her in the Bible and in other books she had read and she recognized them. There was an excitement in Heaven of what was to come, and she knew that God's plan was just beginning to unfold for Heaven and Earth.

In fact, the hype and energy in Heaven was much more exciting than anything she could have ever dreamed up or imagined in her finite mind while living on earth. Earth confined her to her fleshly body. She constantly fought spirits of darkness and they never stopped trying to distort the truth.[29] Suzanne saw unclearly while she lived on earth[30] yet now everything was crystal clear.

Her amazement and reverence for God continued to increase. And the space in heaven was vast and limitless as throngs of those who have inherited salvation were there continuing to do the will of God.

There were the angelic beings who were so massive, beautiful and mighty, yet they used their power only when directed by God. Angels were created to worship God; serve as His messengers to carry out His plan; and to protect His people. They are ministering spirits who are sent to help those who will inherit salvation.[31]

Every time a believer on earth offered up a prayer to God, it was instantly decided how many angels would be needed to fight the battle and win against the principalities and powers of darkness. As long as the prayers continued, it gave the heavenly hosts their direction from God, the angels were dispatched to fight the battle for the believer. It is called spiritual warfare.

As Suzanne learned about her new home, she realized there was a distinct difference in the inhabitants of Heaven. There were angels who constantly went to and fro from the earth. They would begin by escorting souls to earth upon their conception. They would stay with them their entire lifetime, no matter what the length of it was—watching over them every second.

All the days ordained for me were written in your book before one of them came to be.
Psalms 139:16, NIVUK

The angels were servants sent for those who would inherit salvation. Some returned from earth without the life they'd been assigned to watch over.

At such times when an angel returned from earth without the soul it departed with, it was evident to all that the lost soul made the wrong decision. The spiritual battle was lost because that soul surrendered their flesh and their will to sin and darkness, resulting in eternal separation from God.

Next, there were sons and daughters of God— what joy filled Heaven as these believers who lived out their full earthly existence arrived based on their faith in Christ alone.

Each came to Heaven in different ways—through tragedy, illness or sleep; infants, young and old. Each one came with a personal story and different past.

Yet the one, unique experience they held in common was that they individually came to a crossroads of faith and chose to believe in Jesus as their Savior and Lord over their life.

Jesus told him, "I am the way, the truth, and

the life. No one can come to the Father except through me." John 14:6

For this, they inherited eternal life upon their death. They were given the opportunity to choose Jesus by many different paths. Some were told what Jesus did on the Cross by others; some believed through reading God's Word or inspirational books; some believed through seeing God's hand in creation and science; some experienced dreams and visions; others were won by drama, music or videos–all were lead to the Truth. They all made the choice to believe. It was their faith in Jesus that brought them here. Each one entered upon their belief in the blood of Jesus and His death on the Cross. Everyone made it here the same way Suzanne did; not by anything they did or by their own merit, but simply their faith in the blood, death and resurrection of Jesus Christ, the son of God. Some accepted Jesus on their deathbed and did not have a chance to do one good thing. *But Heaven wasn't about goodness, it was about a sacrifice that was already made—not theirs, but Jesus'.* No one could boast about his or her life on earth. They were only here by faith in what Jesus had done for them.

Yet, there was a keen knowledge, too, seeing the *"If only"* of their lives before Christ. What could have been if they'd seen sooner the ultimate plan God laid out for them alone? They would have been able to do so much more for the glory of God while they were still on Earth. Even so, God ordains all; His plan for their lives was always fulfilled in His way and in His time. It is a miraculous wonder just how God works all things for the good of those He loves and calls according to His purpose.[32] And now, in Heaven, there was no judgment or condemnation, just an awe for the redemptive plan God had for each one of them—*woven like a precious tapestry that glorified Him and delighted their soul!*

There were those who brought others with them. Suzanne saw the great cloud of witnesses and recognized many.[33] It was a known fact, but still, there was no boasting. Because the boasting was in Jesus and what He already did—His perfect sacrifice. They all praised God for sending His Son, His gift to man, and they praised Jesus for being willing to go to the cross for them.

Suzanne was again reminded of this passage of Scripture,

> *This is the only work God wants from you:*
> *Believe in the one he has sent.* John 6:29

There was a large group of inhabitants in Heaven who entered between birth and the age of accountability; they died as children in their innocence. They lived a very brief time on earth. They died at birth or a few months or years old—some even still in the womb.

Their lives ended too soon in human terms, but God's love and salvation extends to the womb, and to infants; Jesus received them unto Himself. Each were created with a purpose and fulfilled that purpose. Each were unique and beautiful. When they were presented to Jesus by their guardian angel, Jesus held each one of them in His arms with divine love and comforted each one. They were conceived in a fallen world of sin, with a fallen nature already present at their birth. They may have never committed a willful sin of the flesh but they came in their fallen state due to their ancestors, Adam and Eve. Thus, they were unique from those who willfully committed sin during their lives. Each one understood the plan of redemption.

And then there was a *multitude in Heaven of those who were never allowed to be born*. They were God's creation whom He made for a distinct purpose.[34] They were destroyed in the womb and not given a chance to take their first breath. Their destruction altered God's plan for that unique time in history because they were meant to be born and to live.

God created a plan for these souls to bless the lives of those they would know; some were created to discover cures for diseases; some to be great leaders; some to compose music or create beautiful works of art and some simply to be used in a certain way in a certain person's life. Yet they were destroyed by choice while still in the womb—with no chance to live out the days that God planned for them.

Some of these beautiful children were destroyed by their parents because doctors advised them to do so based on their genetic predisposition. These parents missed the greatest blessing of all, the unconditional love from a child. God knew and planted that child in a womb, however, that child was destroyed out of fear of the unknown, lack of trust or pressure from others.

All those in Heaven were aware of the continual destruction taking place on God's creation and the distortion of His plan. It was a known fact that these unborn souls were increasing very quickly. There was a remarkable difference about them that was clear. Each one possessed the knowledge of who Jesus is and an awareness of their unfulfilled purpose on Earth.

Lastly and mysteriously, there was a hidden place in Heaven. Suzanne realized it was an altar. She saw that under the altar were the souls of all who were martyred for Jesus, God's son. Some there were John the Baptist, Stephen, and most of Jesus' Apostles. They all died for the truth of the Word of God and for being faithful to their testimony. This remained a mystery. They were told to rest a little longer until the full number of their brothers and sisters—*their fellow servants of Jesus who were to be martyred*—joined them, and the number of these were also being added to rapidly and continuously.[35]

These souls had not yet all been revealed to those in Heaven. It was believed by all the inhabitants that it would be soon because the end times on earth were wrapping up. Prophecy was being fulfilled, and the appointed angels were standing at the four corners of the earth with drawn swords, preparing for battle. It was most exciting to know that something big was about to occur, and that hosts of heavenly angels were preparing for a battle. Everyone knew the victor is Jesus. The battle was already won. Jesus would soon judge all and reign forever over His Kingdom and over all Creation.

Suzanne thought the reunions in Heaven were the most exciting thing of all. They took place continuously as loved ones were reunited with one another. The joy was indescribable! The wonder and amazement of those who arrived in Heaven never ended—friends and relatives were astonished at the way a life could be changed from a simple decision to put their faith in Christ and that made the reunions even sweeter.

As Suzanne pondered all of this, the angelic being that escorted her to Heaven—*whom she now knew was her guardian angel the entire time she was on earth*—joined her as she continued along the path. The angel conveyed to Suzanne that he was given a new assignment and he would be leaving Heaven for earth and he had come to bid her goodbye, for now. Walking beside the angel was a little girl who looked so much like Erin that Suzanne was almost confused; yet there is no confusion in heaven.

Immediately, Suzanne knew exactly what was transpiring. The angelic being who was so familiar and knew her so intimately, communicated these words, "I am leaving Heaven to escort this life to earth. I will be gone until her life on earth is over, but Jesus knew you'd want to meet this little girl before she leaves. We are all hoping I will escort her back one day, yet that will depend on her. She's been assigned her purpose and it will be up to her to find and fulfill it, but I will help her and watch over her."

Instantly, Suzanne knew Erin would conceive a child on planet earth that day and in about nine months of earthly time, she would be in a delivery room meeting this little girl. She knelt down and hugged her little granddaughter and said, "Never forget this place, this is your true home—come back to it, Jesus will be waiting for you and so will I."

And then the angel bid Suzanne goodbye. She watched as the angel once again went through the narrow gate to begin the guardianship of a new life— Suzanne's granddaughter named "Grace"—for all the grace that was extended by God to one single person, but is also offered to anyone who will receive it.

> *For it is by grace you have been saved, through faith—and this is not from yourselves, it is the gift of God—not by works, so that no one can boast.* Ephesians 2:8-9, NIV

THE END

"All I have seen teaches me
to trust the Creator
for all I have not seen."

Ralph Waldo Emerson

THE CHOICE

It's been almost forty years
and I still return now and then
To lift up a casket lid
and think about my sin.

There's really not a casket,
a grave or even ashes,
It's just my way of thinking about
a little girl with dark eyelashes.

The first few years I thought
how I was such a fool.
Of all the "firsts" I'd missed,
the "toddler years" and even pre-school.

I still can't believe I listened to
such a big, loud voice,
That said, "Just get rid of it"
and "Exercise your choice."

When it was all over,
it's not like what they said.
Instead, I just kept thinking,
"My little baby is dead."

The years go by, I turn the corner
and there she is again.
I think, "If only I hadn't listened,
she would almost be ten."

Life goes on
and still I visit her in my mind.
I think of an older girl now
whom I'd have taught to be kind.

I'd teach her other things too,
like not to follow the crowd.
I'd tell her to think for herself
and the consequences, for crying out loud!

And then before I know it,
I am middle-aged.
She's there again in my thoughts
and I am filled with rage.

The rage is toward the lie
that was told to me back then.
How if I hadn't listened,
I'd have my daughter now as a friend.

She'd be dreaming of prom dresses, college
and maybe even a boy.
I'd be thinking happier thoughts than these,
and she would bring me joy.

I must forget about these things
because she will not be there,
And other things too,
like the the color of her hair.

Forget about her eyes,
were they brown or green or blue?
I truly wonder about all of this;
do you wonder about it too?

I thought of a wedding once and
how so very much she's missed.
Maybe there's a boy out there
who would have been her first kiss.

It wasn't her decision
to never take one breath;
I decided for her back then,
and sadly I chose death.

I am over fifty now
and my mind still turns toward her.
She'd be a grown woman now
and her company I'd prefer.

Sometimes in my mind,
she's carrying a load in her arms.
She's smiling, laughing and running
with lots of grace and charm.

She's bringing me a gift,
something she wants me to see.
It's her little baby she's so proud of,
and he's looking up at me.

Because a baby truly is a gift,
not to be thrown away,
In plastic bags or garbage cans
and discarded in just one day.

They're little gifts from God,
children He wanted to bless us with,
But instead of being thankful,
we believed a deadly myth.

The myth that they're not babies—
just blobs and skin and cells.
We let doctors suck them out of us
and then we never tell.

And now as I think about
how almost forty years have gone by,
I will never, ever forget those lies,
no matter how hard I try.

(Poem by author)

You made all the delicate,
inner parts of my body
and knit me together in my mother's womb.

Thank you for making me so wonderfully complex!
Your workmanship is marvelous—
how well I know it.

You watched me as I was being formed
in utter seclusion, as I was woven together
in the dark of the womb.

You saw me before I was born.
Every day of my life was recorded in your book.
Every moment was laid out
before a single day had passed.

Psalms 139:13-16

ENDNOTES

1. Matthew 7:14, p. 61

2. Revelation 22:5, p. 62

3. Revelation 4:3-4, p. 63

4. Revelation 4:5, p. 63

5. Revelation 5:8, p. 63

6. Revelation 22:1-2, p. 63

7. Revelation 4:8, p. 63

8. 1 Corinthians 13:12, p. 64

9. *For we know that when this earthly tent we live in is taken down (that is, when we die and leave this earthly body), we will have a house in Heaven, an eternal body made for us by God himself and not by human hands* (2 Corinthians 5:1), p. 68

10. *They will walk with me in white, for they are worthy. All who are victorious will be clothed in white. I will never erase their names from the Book of Life, but I will announce before my Father and his angels that they are mine* (Revelation 3:4-5), p. 68

11. *We, too, wait with eager hope for the day when God will give us our full rights as his adopted children, including the new bodies he has promised us. We were given this hope when we were saved* (Romans 8:23-24), p. 68

12. *But one thing I do: Forgetting what is behind and straining toward what is ahead* (Philippians 3.13, NIV), p. 113

13. 1 Corinthians 12:27, p. 114

14. *Therefore confess your sins to each other and pray for each other so that you may be healed. The prayer of a righteous person is powerful and effective* (James 5:16, NIV), p. 134

15. *If we confess our sins, he is faithful and just to forgive us our sins and to cleanse us from all unrighteousness* (1 John 1:9, ESV), p. 135

16. *So if the Son sets you free, you are truly free* (John 8:36), p. 135

17. *The bread of God is the bread that comes down from Heaven. He gives life to the world* (John 6:33, ESV), p. 138

18. *So now there is no condemnation for those who belong to Christ Jesus* (Romans 8:1), p. 139

19. *… The one who accuses them before our God day and night* (Revelation 12:10), p. 139

20. *For we are not fighting against flesh-and-blood enemies, but against evil rulers and authorities of the unseen world, against mighty powers in this dark world, and against evil spirits in the Heavenly places* (Ephesians 6:12), p. 139

21. *As the Scriptures say, No one is righteous—not even one* (Romans 3:10), p. 153

22. *Jesus told them, "This is the only work God wants from you: Believe in the one he has sent"* (John 6:29), p. 154

23. *Then you will experience God's peace, which exceeds anything we can understand. His peace will guard your heart and minds as you live in Christ Jesus* (Philippians 4:7), p. 154

24. Psalms 127:3, p. 162

25. *For all that is secret will eventually be brought into the open, and everything that is concealed will be brought to light and made known to all* (Luke 8:17), p. 173

26. Romans 8:1, p. 177

27. John 14:2, p. 179

28. Hebrews 11:1, p. 188

29. *Our fight is not against human beings. It is against the rulers, the authorities and the powers of this dark world. It is against the spiritual forces of evil in the Heavenly world* (Ephesians 6:12, NIRV), p. 190

30. *Now we see only a dim likeness of things. It is as if we were seeing them in a foggy mirror. But someday we will see clearly. We will see face to face. What I know now is not complete. But someday I will know completely, just as God knows me completely* (1 Corinthians 13:12, NIRV), p. 190

31. *Therefore, angels are only servants—spirits sent to care for people who will inherit salvation* (Hebrews 1:14), p. 190

32. Romans 8:28, p. 193

33. Hebrews 12:1, p. 193

34. *Before I formed you in the womb I knew you, before you were born I set you apart* (Jeremiah 1:5, NIV), p. 194

35. Revelation 6:9-11, p. 195